A novel
Adapted from the ~~.....~~ ~~.....~~

VAMPYRES

☼

STREGA

The right of Tim Greaves to be identified as the author of this work
has been asserted by him in accordance with the Copyright, Designs
and Patents Act 1988

First published in June 2001 by
Strega
An imprint of FAB Press
PO Box 178, Guildford, Surrey, GU3 2YU, England, UK

www.fabpress.com/strega/

A CIP catalogue record for this book is available from the
British Library

ISBN 1-903254-11-6

CONTENTS

ACKNOWLEDGEMENTS

Special thanks to José Ramon Larraz for his kind assistance and support, Brian Smedley-Aston for providing us with original stills from the film 'Vampyres', and Deborah Bacci for the Strega logo.

FOREWORD

I find this novelisation by Tim Greaves an exciting work of fiction, a story of "infinite horror". He is undoubtedly a connoisseur of the supernatural and the bizarre. As such this is not a book to be read on a stormy night if you do not want to suffer nightmares!

Tim has managed to create an atmosphere that I have rarely encountered in other tales of vampires - he mixes fantasy, fear, sensuality and reality in a way that captivates because it convinces. I now believe that if it had been possible to read his interpretation of my story before shooting 'Vampyres', the film would have been greatly enriched.

Read on and relish...

José Ramon Larraz
November 2000

I

LOVE AND DEATH

The serenity of the English countryside in autumn is a
remarkable thing. In those few weeks as September turns to
October, leaving in its wake the last vestiges of summer -
warm, scented air adopting a crisp chill, lush greens turning
to murky browns, fragrant life withering to stale death - it
can be as tranquil a landscape in which to immerse oneself
as can be found anywhere in the world. To while away an
hour or two strolling through an autumn woodland whilst
contemplating nothing more cerebral than what a pleasure it
is to be alive, is an indulgence upon which there can be no
price. Indeed, roaming the woods that circumvent the
grounds of Farnsworth Hall, deep in the north Hampshire
countryside, is tantamount to what it might have been like to
visit the Garden of Eden.

But then even the Garden of Eden was tainted by sin.

✻

In spite of the hypnotic glow with which the full, ivory
orb of the moon gilded the vast acreage that constituted the
grounds of Farnsworth Hall, the indefinably sinister edifice
itself remained in blackness. The lofty perimeter fauna cast
bold, inky shadows that prevented even the narrowest shaft
of illumination from touching upon its weather-beaten grey
stone.

Hidden within the undergrowth some creature or other
was busy foraging for its meal. Somewhere off in the dense
woods at the back of the house a pair of nightingales were
engaged in a ritual of courtship, their chittery-chattering
eclipsed by the monotone hooting of an owl. But for these
sounds, barely audible from the enclosure that fronted the
house, the frosty night air was as silent as the grave.

The truth of the matter was that no-one in their right mind would have been caught in the vicinity of Farnsworth Hall after dark. Even by day it was a unnerving spot. There are houses like Farnsworth everywhere. It was one of those places that children will nervously dare each other to approach; which one would be brave enough to go right up to the front door and, bolder yet, knock the knocker and run? The - admittedly slightly uncertain - knowledge that no-one would actually answer made no difference where Farnsworth was concerned; fundamental animal fear made even those who feigned the most convincing bravado loathe to actually make good on their bluster. For there is rarely smoke without fire and the fact is that Farnsworth Hall had a history that local people would sooner forget.

It had been close to two hundred years since a wealthy physician, one Dr. Terence Farnsworth, had financed its construction as a private institute for the study of the mentally deficient. Within its first year of opening stories had spread through the nearby village that heinous cruelties were being carried out there. Transients who had slept rough in the woods that encircled the grounds told stories of horrible screams in the dark of the night. Eventually, accused of the most unspeakable acts of barbarity, Farnsworth came under investigation. He swore that his methods were both scientific and humane, but a trial and, worse still, a scandal seemed inevitable.

One morning he was found naked, hanging by the cord of his robe from one of the banisters in the east wing. The official verdict was suicide, but the popular belief was that one of the good Dr. Farnsworth's less than stable patients had taken it upon himself to exact a little retribution.

Farnsworth Hall was closed and, soiled by the stories of depravity that had taken place there, remained empty until the early 1900's when, via a legal loophole, it was purchased by the county for a figure well below its potential value. A short while later it was open again, now a nursing home for the elderly. In the decades that followed, many aged souls passed through its corridors on their way to meet their maker.

There is no disputing that, in all manner of ways, Farnsworth Hall had seen more than its fair share of death.

After a fire that was never explained, in which a great many of the staff and residents perished, Farnsworth once again closed its doors and remained that way for some years, skirting several threats of demolition.

In the late 1960's a fly by night Lancastrian entrepreneur named Trent bought the house and its grounds for a pittance with the wild notion of turning it into some sort of theme park. He took up residence in the east wing and set about bringing his plans to fruition. Then, having heard nothing from him in weeks, his daughter, Miriam, arrived one night and discovered the stinking corpse with its throat slashed wide from ear to ear; Trent had been dead for more than a week. There was talk of felonious connections and excessive gambling debts, but the murder went unsolved and in the village they preferred to believe it was something more supernatural. As far as most people were concerned, Farnsworth Hall was cursed.

Miriam Trent retained ownership of the property but had no wish to live there on a permanent basis. She would occasionally be seen passing through the village in her flashy little sports car, more often than not in the company of a female acquaintance. She would stay up at the house for a day or two, and then disappear back to wherever it was she had come from.

And so it was that the house remained empty, in spite of attempts by a number of interested parties to cajole Miriam to sell. It would be fair to say, however, that the sound of human activity was something of which Farnsworth had, in the main, been devoid for more than three years.

＊

This particular evening, were it not for the dim luminescence radiating from the window of one of the upstairs rooms, the casual observer would have seen no evidence to suggest that the house was inhabited, or indeed had been at all since the unpleasant Trent business. Inside, its unlit hallways and countless rooms, stale with the acrid scent of decay, were meagrely furnished and everything was coated with a liberal film of long-undisturbed dust.

Then, somewhere within the recesses of Farnsworth Hall, a clock chimed one.

By stark contrast to the rest of the house, the bedroom located in the east wing, lit only by the dim bulb of a table lamp, was bedecked in the most admirable decor. The floorboards were bare, yet polished and buffed to a golden lustre; the plain white walls bore a collection of exquisite framed prints, each depicting an image of Victorian erotica, which even a novice would be hard pressed not to recognise would fetch something in the six figure bracket were they to come to auction; the wine red velvet curtains were embroidered with the finest silver thread.

Against the back wall, languishing upon a king size bed, were two naked women, their limbs entwined in urgent embrace. The taller of the pair, Francesca, her mane of chestnut tresses splayed out across silk pillows, shifted her slender frame a little to get more comfortable as the smaller girl, the flaxen-haired Miriam Trent, peppered her neck and shoulders with tiny butterfly kisses. With the edges of her teeth she nibbled gently at the lobes of Fran's ears, eliciting small intakes of breath from her lover.

'I want you', Miriam murmured, the feel of her warm, whispery breath sending a frisson of pleasure coursing through Fran's body.

Francesca smiled up into her companion's ice blue eyes.

'Kiss me.'

Their mouths met with an intense passion, lips parting, tongues exploring. Fran trembled as her lover kissed lightly across her throat, moving downwards and coming to rest poised over the soft, rounded, inviting warmth of her breast. When the tip of Miriam's tongue began to flick gently around the large, flawless dark circle of the areola, Fran felt a tingling in the pit of her stomach as the nipple grew hard. Her sighs of pleasure became gasps of excitement as she felt one of Miriam's cool hands trail over her thighs, long nails scratching - oh, so delicately - in circular motions across the creamy flesh. Almost involuntarily Fran parted her legs to permit Miriam freedom of access to the sweet, burning wetness that dwelled there.

The soft footsteps echoing on the stairwell were almost imperceptible, but absorbed in their swelling rapture, neither Fran nor Miriam would have been likely to have heard them anyway.

The rubber-soled shoes moved swiftly but discreetly through darkness that was penetrated only by a glimmer of light emanating from beneath the solid oak door. The owner of the feet stopped short of the door and remained stock still for a full minute, breathing in short, controlled bursts through his nostrils, listening to the muffled sounds of pleasure coming from within.

Fran's moaning grew louder as Miriam's expert fingers teased her, bringing her to the threshold of orgasm, and then easing back, waiting for the moment to pass before resuming her ministrations.

'I love you, Miriam', Francesca whispered breathlessly, bucking her hips in rhythmic circles in co-ordination with each thrust of her sweetheart's fingers.

Neither girl heard the hushed twisting of the ornate doorknob.

All the while Miriam's mouth continued its rotation of duty, moving from the flat of Fran's stomach, up over the full, heaving breasts, across the warm, pulsing gooseflesh of the neck, brushing softly over the moist lips, and then back down again.

A floorboard creaked, or maybe the sound came from the hinges of the door.

Miriam spun round and sat bolt upright as she saw the heavy door swing wide. A figure, swathed in black, his features hidden beneath the shadow of a broad-rimmed fedora, took a single stride into the room.

What happened next was over in a matter of perhaps fifteen seconds, yet for the defenceless girls the whole gruesome incident felt as if it were happening in a surreal slow-motion, like everything around them were part of some crazy film being projected on an out-of-control movieola that had suddenly slowed down to a quarter of the necessary running speed.

As Fran scrabbled to draw the blankets over her nakedness, Miriam was executing that classic manoeuvre of female modesty; one arm flew up across her breasts while her hand flashed downward to conceal her crotch. At the same time the delicate chiselled features contorted into an expression of stark terror as her eyes fell upon the long barrel of the gun - clutched firmly in the black-gloved hand of the intruder - pointing directly at her.

Miriam tried to get up, oblivious to the fact that the screaming pounding through her ears was her own. The half-inch-wide black hole stared at her malevolently and then promptly spat out its first word. The bullet struck home just beneath Miriam's ribcage. Fran was struggling to get off the bed as the second bullet impacted with her sternum, propelling her back against the headboard. She shrieked in pain as the third bullet found its mark in her left breast.

Miriam was gasping for breath as white hot pain seared through her abdomen. She gazed down at the small red hole, almost unable to comprehend the sight of the dark fluid seeping out across her stomach. She turned her head and looked into Fran's eyes - only moments earlier burning with desire, now wet with tears - and the unspoken message they conveyed was a precise reflection of the words howling through her head. Resounding, over and over: *We're going to die, we're going to die, we're going...*

Her mouth dribbling blood, Miriam lurched forward and managed to get her feet on the floor. As she stood, she threw out her hands in front of her in a futile gesture of self-preservation. The fourth and fifth bullets showed as little mercy as those that had preceded them; one struck the poor girl in the shoulder, the other passed straight through the palm of her right hand and planted itself firmly in her cheek. Her blue eyes gaped wide and the lips smeared with red twitched, trying to form a single word - 'Why?' - but no sound came out.

A split second later the sixth bullet drew a blessed veil over her agony, finding its target directly between the eyes. Miriam's head flew back, the front of her skull shattered and a spray of red mist spewed upwards as she pitched sideways, dead before she even hit the floor.

Fran was now sobbing uncontrollably, the tears burning her cheeks as she tried desperately to understand the indistinct words that echoed through her head. And where the hell were they coming from?

'Please, no. Please. Don't kill me.'

In the last few seconds of her life, through a sea of pain, Fran thought that she recognised that voice, so very, very far away. It sounded curiously like her own. How banal, she thought, that she should not have known her own voice. And she hadn't even spoken... had she? She didn't think so, but...

...there were no words that would have made a difference anyway. The barrel kicked twice as the final messengers of death, one directly on the tail of the other, traversed the few yards between the assailant and his victim. One tore into Fran's throat and, as her hand shot up and clutched at the wound, the second signed her death warrant, puncturing the centre of her heart. She collapsed back onto sheets sodden with blood, her head lolled to one side and her eyes stared, unseeing, at the prone body of Miriam, that beautiful fair skin lacerated and streaked with red.

The man stood in the doorway, the silence that had fallen in the room broken only by his now less controlled breathing. The eyes moved slowly back and forth across the carnage, surveying the results of his unsolicited visit. Blood. Everywhere blood. And two lifeless bodies that only moments earlier had been radiant, happy, living, breathing people. Francesca Morris and Miriam Trent were dead.

Asked for it. Deserved it. Fuckin' lezzie bitches.

The killer swallowed twice and steadied himself against the door frame, choking back an urge to vomit and waiting for the adrenaline rush to subside.

15

Then, as stealthily as he had arrived, he gently pulled the door shut, stepped back into the ebony blackness and, like a will-o'-the-wisp, disappeared into the night.

II

ANOTHER TIME, ANOTHER PLACE

The BMW, tyres squealing and metallic blue paintwork glinting in the mid-afternoon sun, roared into the gravelled forecourt of the Wayfarer Inn as if it were being pursued by an E-Type Jaguar driven by the devil himself. Radio blaring, the car swerved just in time to avoid the stone effigy of a man on horseback standing proudly in the centre of the otherwise unoccupied forecourt. The driver braked hard and the car slewed to the left, spitting up chippings and coming to an abrupt halt parallel to the twin lines of flower beds.

Seated behind the wheel, Ted Gorman pulled a large white handkerchief from the breast pocket of his fashionable brown tweed jacket and briskly mopped his face. It was an unusually warm afternoon. For October anyway.

'Shit!', he said.

I don't remember that thing being there last time.

Winding down the window, Ted leant out and looked back at the statue.

'Oh, I don't know,' he muttered, 'maybe it was.'

Scowling, he reached down to switch off the radio - '...and that was the new number one, John Denver with "Annie's Song"...' - then pulled an unopened carton of 20 Rothmans from his jacket pocket. Slitting the cellophane wrapper with his thumbnail, he withdrew one and lit it with his monogrammed Ronson lighter, its shiny black glaze finish worn with use. He'd sought out and bought the lighter almost fifteen years previously after reading in a Fleming novel that James Bond owned one. Sure, it was pretentious, but he loved to flash it at parties and tell people it was just like the one used by the great Double-O-Seven himself. It was an effective ice-breaker and rarely failed to impress the ladies. And Ted was expert at impressing the ladies. Besides which, the Ronson had proven a sound purchase, for it worked as well now as the day it was new.

Ted inhaled deeply and sighed out a long, thin plume of smoke that drifted up and out of the window. It had been all of three years since he had last set foot in this place. If it had been twenty years it would have been too soon.

For some reason that, beyond tiredness and being back here, he was unable to pinpoint, Ted felt positively irritable. He often felt that way. And as a result of not knowing why, he tended to become even more fractious. It was a vicious circle.

Taking two more quick puffs on his cigarette, Ted stubbed out the hardly used remains in the ashtray. He wound up the window, leant over and pulled his briefcase from the back seat, then climbed out of the car. Locking up, he pocketed the keys and casually sauntered over to The Wayfarer, pausing to read the chalkboard sign on the wall by the entrance.

THE WAYFARER WELCOMES YOU

it said in bold red capital letters. Then below, in smaller, neat white lettering:

Premium draught ales available in our newly refurbished
lounge bar

And below that, smaller still:

Excellent cuisine served lunchtimes and evenings in our brasserie
- a real taste of Hampshire

In the space at the bottom, beneath the heading "Today's Special", someone had written in less than tidy white chalk scrawl :

Cream of Onion Soup
Braised Venison
Creme Brulee
Coffee
- only £3.49

Suddenly Ted felt hungry. He pushed open the glass swing doors and walked inside.

It was as if he had stepped into a time warp. It might have been three years since Ted had last been inside the lobby of The Wayfarer, but it hadn't changed a bit. The same worn lime green carpet, the highly polished oak panelling lining the walls, the sickly sweet scent of potpourri - fresh out of an aerosol canister - hanging in the air. No, nothing had changed.

Nothing?

Ted looked approvingly at the pretty, dark-haired girl stood behind the reception desk. Well, not quite nothing; the hired help was a definite improvement on his last visit.

He walked across the lobby and set down his briefcase. The girl looked up and smiled, hastily tucking the well-thumbed copy of "Emmanuelle" out of sight beneath the desk.

'Good afternoon, sir.'

Could she have looked or sounded any less interested? How old was she? Seventeen maybe? Eighteen at most.

The fixed smile was as phoney as the oak panelling on the walls.

'Can I help you?'

No, I just thought I'd come and stand in your lobby like a moron, Ted thought.

He said, politely: 'Yes please, er..', he glanced at the nametag, '...Paula. Could I have a room for the night?'

'Single?'

'Yes please, with a bath if possible.'

The girl fumbled about underneath the counter, withdrew a registration form and slid it over towards Ted. She set down a cartridge pen on the top.

'If you'd just like to fill in this form. Name and address.'

Ted removed the top from the pen but, as he pressed the nib to the paper, a blob of ink seeped out.

Shit!

'I'm afraid the dining room closed an hour ago,' the girl said.

'What?', Ted snapped, scowling.

The smile dropped from the girl's face. Slightly taken aback by Ted's rather brusque tone, she giggled nervously, 'I was joking. I heard you arrive. I, er... I thought you sounded in a bit of a hurry, like maybe you couldn't wait to taste today's special.'

The poor girl was squirming. Ted immediately felt bad.

'Oh, I see.' His scowl vanished, replaced by the winning Gorman smile. 'No, I er...Well, I'm very tired. I wasn't paying attention and almost drove right past you.' Ted winked. 'Took the old corner a bit fast.'

The girl's face resumed it's well-practiced "always be sure to smile at the patrons" expression. Ted had the pen poised over the dateline at the top of the page.

'It's Tuesday the 15th,' the girl prompted.

'Thanks.'

As Ted returned his attention to the form, an elderly man in a dark blue suit stepped out from a door at the back - upon which was mounted an oblong plaque that said 'Manager' - and leant on the reception desk. He was peering at Ted over the top of his rimless spectacles.

'The gentleman's an old client,' he said to the girl.

Ted looked up sharply. The man was smiling pleasantly at him, revealing a mouth full of crooked, yellowed teeth.

'We haven't seen you down here for years,' the old man continued. 'Hmmm, my word, yes. Years have gone by since then.'

He stopped as he realised that Ted was frowning at him.

'Do you remember me?' the old man asked.

Shaking his head, Ted said, 'I'm sorry, no', and went back to filling in the requisite details on the form. For reasons he didn't wish to discuss, or for that matter even think about, Ted had no desire to retread the memories of his last stopover at The Wayfarer.

'I'm positive I've seen you here before,' the old man persisted, his gimlet eyes performing a wordless interrogation.

Clenching his teeth, Ted tried to focus on the registration form. Without looking up, he said, firmly, 'I'm afraid you're mistaken.'

Had that sounded sincere? Did he look as shifty as he felt? Would his eyes betray him?

Ted kept his head down. The man looked a little crestfallen.

'I'm sorry,' he said, 'I must have confused you with someone else.'

Ted finished filling out the form, scribbled his signature at the bottom and handed the pen back to the girl. She took it from him, deftly filed the paperwork, and then lifted up the hinged flap on the counter. She stepped out past Ted, revealing as she did so a very shapely pair of legs beneath a mini skirt so obscenely short that a tantalising glimpse of white briefs stretched taut across nubile crotch was unavoidable.

''I'll show you to your room,' she said. 'Do you have some luggage?'

'No, none,' Ted replied, picking up his briefcase and following the girl across the lobby to the stairs.

A puzzled expression on his face, the old man went back into his office and shut the door. He'd been so sure.

Why on earth should the gentleman not wish to be remembered?

✳

The girl let Ted into a small, brightly decorated room on the first floor and handed him the key.

'Is there anything else I can do for you, sir?'

Aside from coming in here and letting me see if what you have hidden under those pretty little clothes lives up to its suggested succulence?

'No thanks,' Ted said. Then: 'Oh, wait a minute. Would it be possible to have a bottle of wine sent up? Anything will do, as long as it's red, wet and cheap.' He winked.

'Certainly,' the girl nodded and turned to leave.

'Actually,' Ted added, 'make it two bottles would you?'

Unseen by Ted, the girl raised an eyebrow but said simply: 'Of course. I'll have them sent up right away.' She hurried off down the hall.

Ted shut the door and dropped his briefcase on the bed.

Was that the hint of a come-hither smile?... Oh, for heaven's sake, man, stop massaging your own ego. She's half your age!

Being a salesman was beginning to lose its appeal. A few years back it wouldn't have even crossed Ted's mind how much time he spent on the road every week. He'd drive hundreds of miles just to close a deal. It wasn't being vainglorious either. He'd been a first class go-getting bastard, never once turning his back on a challenge. The bigger the better in fact. Ever striving - and usually succeeding - in getting a signature on that contract. So what if his methods weren't always ethical? Ethics didn't come into it. Howard & Sons weren't interested in the hows and whys. He might be all high and mighty on the face of it, but old man Howard would readily turn a blind eye to just about anything as long as the job got done. And, by God, Ted Gorman got the job done. That was why they paid him so well. Yes indeed. What was it that Ebenzer Scrooge said to Marley's Ghost? 'You were always a good man of business,' Ted said aloud to the empty room.

But what about life? Not quite such a success story there, is it old son?

An expensive, beautifully decorated and furnished house was all very well, but it was a hell of a lonely place to return to after a business trip without a woman waiting with the home fires burning. For a little while Ted had even thought he'd got that bit right too... until the bitch upped and walked out on him. And why? Because she'd fallen for...

There was knock at the door and the wine arrived. Ted thanked the girl, slipped her a fifty pence piece and closed the door.

It was all too painful to think about. 'Oh, Ghost of Ted's Life Past,' he mumbled, bastardising his beloved Dickens as he pulled the corks from the two bottles. 'Why do you delight to torture me? Show me no more!'

Ted stood in front of the mirror in his room and carefully applied two drops of cleansing solution into each of his eyes. Blinking away the residue, he studied the face that stared back at him from the glass.

A combination of the years and the mileage was taking its toll. Not only did Ted look every bit his 38 years, he felt them... and a few more besides. He ran a hand around his jaw-line.

Could use a shave.

The once taught skin on his face was no longer quite so taught and what once had been a flawless complexion was now showing worrying signs of stress. Worst of all, when he smiled, those little crow's feet things appeared at the edges of his eyes.

Bloody crow's feet, for Christ's sake! And as for the hair...

What not so long ago had been a luxuriant mop of jet black was now flecked with grey and thinning with alarming rapidity. Distinguished, some people called it. That certainly wasn't what Ted called it. Old was what Ted called it.

Maybe it was time to think about doing something else. Time to move on. The money was good with Howard & Sons, but he had been smart enough to stash away quite a nest egg in the past year or two and he wasn't daft. He could turn his hand to just about anything he chose. Finding something new, something fresh and more interesting shouldn't be hard for Ted Gorman.

'Insurrection,' he said aloud. Then - his voice taking on a not particularly accurate approximation of the phlegmy tones of his employer - he added: 'This won't do at all, old son. Oh no, no, no. It most assuredly will not. The Board simply won't stand for it!'

Ted smiled to himself. To hell with it. At least he had pulled off the Coleman deal. He could walk out with his head held high. He was still the blue-eyed boy as far as old man Howard was concerned.

The smile faded. If only the Coleman deal hadn't brought him back into this neck of the woods. Sure, Ted hadn't *had* to stop off here, but he was dog tired and The Wayfarer used to serve up the best steak dinner within fifty miles. And, fingers crossed, it still did. He'd eat well tonight, be up in time for a leisurely breakfast in the morning, and be on the road again by ten.

Ted filled a glass from the first bottle of wine and swallowed it in three gulps. He stretched, then poured another, filling the glass to the brim. It really was the most appalling stuff. He glanced at his watch. At least three hours before the dining room would be serving. Time enough to cross the t's and dot the i's on the Coleman report and grab a short nap.

He drew the chartreuse curtains together and then, locking the door - more from force of habit than as a precursor to anything of an especially furtive nature - Ted perched himself on the edge of the bed and opened his briefcase.

III

FROM BEYOND THE GRAVE

Within an hour of Ted Gorman slipping into untroubled slumber in the arms of Morpheus, outside the Wayfarer Inn the temperature had receded to something much more in keeping with the time of year.

Five miles away John and Harriet Bailey were seeking somewhere to pull over for the night. With caravan in tow, John carefully negotiated the white Wolseley through each bend in the narrow, winding, tree-lined lane.

Pressure of work in the city and business overseas had conspired to keep John's vacation time to a minimum the past year or two and he'd for some time been promising Harriet that they would have a decent break away together. He had finally brought pressure to bear at the office - it wasn't, after all, as if he was demanding anything he wasn't long overdue - and the best part of a month of freedom from the trials of everyday living lay ahead of them. Headed for nowhere in particular, they were getting their first holiday away for several years. The first since their honeymoon in fact.

Harriet had made no secret of the fact that she would have preferred somewhere hot - Barbados and Martinique had been mentioned - and money certainly hadn't been the obstacle. But the reality of it was that John felt that he spent more than enough time in the air and was keen to get out on the open road with the caravan. They had often spent weekends away camping before they were married, but the caravan had sat unemployed in the driveway since he'd picked it up cheaply through an ad in the local paper at the beginning of the year. It was in desperate need of an airing, and John had a hankering to do a little fishing too. He had argued that the time and energy getting to and returning from some distant tropical paradise negated any of the real pleasure and relaxation to be gained from being there. And there was so much of their own soil that had yet to be explored.

In spite of herself, Harriet sort of knew he was right and the bottom line was that as long as they were together she didn't really mind where the destination was. So she had relented and now here they were. With John's driving and Harriet's expert navigation they had leisurely crossed three counties in two days. The first night's stop had admittedly been less than successful when they had been kept awake for most of the night by a herd of cows in a neighbouring field. But the second night was far more restful and Harriet had slept as soundly as she could remember having done in a very long while.

The present plan of action was to find somewhere pleasant where they could set up camp and take root for a few days.

'It's getting dark already,' John remarked.

Harriet looked out at the gloomy sky ahead of them. 'Yeah, well, those rain clouds aren't helping much, are they? It looks like the heavens are just about ready to split.'

John grinned. 'Ever the optimist,' he said. 'Take a look at the map will you? See where we are.'

Harriet leant forward and opened the glove compartment. Inside was a small collection of Ordnance Survey maps charting different areas of the British Isles. She pulled out the top three, selected the one she needed and slipped the others back, snapping the glove compartment shut. As she began to unfold the map, she spotted something by the roadside about a hundred yards ahead of them that made her stop what she was doing for a moment.

As the Wolseley got closer a woman, clad in a black gown and a long black velvet cape lined with vivid purple silk draped around her shoulders, stepped from behind the trees. The face was indistinct in the late afternoon shadows, but as the car drew level and Harriet turned her head to look, their eyes met and she could almost feel the mystery woman's stare burning into her. At the last moment, as they passed by, a small movement in the undergrowth behind the woman caught Harriet's eye. She saw - or at least *thought* she saw - a second woman, dressed similarly except for the lining of the cloak which was the deepest scarlet, crouched low among the trees. As if she were trying to avoid being seen.

How odd.

'Did you see that woman?' John asked absent-mindedly.

'Two,' Harriet corrected him.

'I only saw one.'

Harriet shook her head. 'No, there was another one. She was behind the trees.'

'Really?', John responded, making no effort to disguise the note of sarcasm that might as well have supplemented the question with: *'...and was she wearing a trapeze dress and juggling live monkeys?'*

Harriet ignored his tone. 'I'm sure she was hiding.'

John glanced at her affectionately and smiled. 'Aside from that stop-off at lunchtime we've been in the car all day, darling. I think perhaps you're getting a little stir crazy and starting to hallucinate.'

'No.' Harriet was adamant. 'I'm sure.' She scowled at John. She loved him to bits, but he could say some bloody asinine things sometimes.

Whether she had seen anything or not, this was a conversation that could easily develop into a petty squabble, and one which John knew he wouldn't win. Best to nip it in the bud straight away.

'Well, let's leave it that I saw one, you saw two. If she - or they,' he added hastily, *'are* hitch-hikers, someone's bound to give them a lift.'

As the words left his lips, several hundred yards back up the road behind them a car slowed down and stopped alongside the mystery woman who, as anyone who had known her would swear, was the spitting image of Francesca Morris... one of the bodies that had been discovered shot dead nearby some three years earlier.

'Could you give me a lift?' she asked. 'It's not very far.'

The driver of the car would have escorted this vision of loveliness to the ends of the earth if she'd asked him to.

'Sure,' he said. 'Hop in.'

The woman who looked like Fran swept around to the other side of the car and slipped gracefully into the passenger seat.

'Thanks very much,' she smiled sweetly.

Lurking among the trees beside the road, a blonde haired girl - as much the spitting image of the deceased Miriam Trent as the other woman was of Francesca Morris - watched as the car accelerated away down the road, gathering speed and disappearing round the bend. She hesitated for a moment, sniffing warily at the air like a animal in a state of nervous excitement trying to make sure that it was safe to make a move. Her breath struck the cold air in a series of tiny puffs. Then, deciding that the coast was clear, she scurried across the small clearing and evanesced into the thick of the woods which, on the far side, about half a mile away, opened out onto the grounds of Farnsworth Hall.

✻

The light was fading rapidly now. John switched on the headlights and the twin beams pierced the gathering darkness on the road in front of them. Spotting a turning to the left a little way ahead, he lightly touched the brakes and they slowed to a crawl. Through the thicket of trees, in the distance John thought he could see water and what looked like a piece of open ground. They stopped at the junction.

'This looks like it could well be the spot,' he said. 'It's getting too dark to go much further tonight anyway.'

Turning the wheel hard to the left, he steered off the road and immediately wished he'd thought twice about it; they were travelling something that was hardly more than a muddy track. The Wolseley nosed its way gingerly through the dense overhanging branches, which brushed across the windscreen and scratched at the roof. Occasionally one of the back wheels lost its grip and spun free for a moment or two, kicking up a filthy spray that caked the wings of the caravan. But then, just as John thought they might be in trouble, the wheel would bite home and they would be on the move again.

'Good choice, darling,' Harriet said with a forced smile. 'I hope we don't wind up getting stuck. We're in the middle of bloody nowhere and *I'm* not walking out of here to find a tow truck.'

John laughed. He was getting worried himself, though he'd never admit to it. 'Oh, yea of little faith.'

They proceeded down the track for about another forty yards and then suddenly the branches subsided and they were pulling into a leafy clearing amidst the trees. Far off to the right, the last rays of the setting sun glittered on the surface of a lake.

'Perfect,' John sighed. 'Absolutely perfect. The only guests here this evening will be Mr. and Mrs. Bailey and their trusty jalopy'

'Er, not quite,' Harriet corrected him. She pointed: 'What about that house over there? This is probably private property.'

John spun the wheel, and the Wolseley turned in an arc and came to a standstill on a stretch of grass at the edge of the trees. He squinted through the dusk at the immense, Gothic-looking shape of Farnsworth Hall.

'Looks abandoned to me. Don't worry. If our being here is a problem for anyone I'm sure we'll hear about it soon enough.'

✳

Thirty minutes later, the appetising scent of frying food was wafting out through the slatted window at the kitchenette end of the caravan. They ate without speaking. Lunch had comprised a couple of cheese and pickle rolls, and now both Harriet and John were far hungrier than they had realised. Only after the bacon, sausage and scrambled eggs had been consumed, and Harriet had set down large mugs of hot, sweet tea on the fold-out table, did John break the silence.

Stretching out on the sofa, he lit a cigarette and leant back against the patchwork cushions. 'Well, we've certainly covered a good distance in the last few days,' he mused.

Harriet had seated herself back down at the table and was gazing into her tea, idly twisting her long brown hair around the middle finger of her left hand. 'Yes, we have,' she said absent-mindedly.

John knew from the fiddling with the hair that something was preying on her mind. 'What's the matter?' he asked.

Harriet seemed surprised by the question. 'With me? Nothing.'

'Come on,' John persevered. 'You sounded a million miles away just now, and you look worried.'

Giving a little involuntary shiver, Harriet wrapped her arms around her shoulders and rubbed them briskly. 'Oh, I don't know, it's silly, but...' She paused, trying to decide whether or not she should speak her mind. 'This place frightens me.'

John laughed. 'It's not the first time we've camped in the woods. I think we're both tired. You'll be more cheerful after a night's sleep.'

Harriet nodded, but she wasn't so sure she was going to sleep at all. She had an uncomfortable sensation in the pit of her stomach. It was a feeling that was all too familiar. It was never anything she could define, but invariably that feeling was a portent of something unpleasant and she had become both wary and respectful of it.

John sipped at his tea. 'I think I'll go down to the lake tomorrow and see if there are any fish.'

Harriet wasn't listening. She sat staring into her mug and continued twiddling her hair. 'Why should one of them be hiding behind a tree?' she said, thinking aloud.

John frowned. 'What?'

Harriet repeated herself and John rolled his eyes towards the heavens. 'I told you,' he began, 'I didn't see anyone hiding.'

Standing up and walking to the sink, Harriet said, 'Well I did. One woman was standing on the edge of the road, the other one was hiding in the woods watching for something. Perhaps just waiting...' She emptied the last of her tea into the sink and washed it away.

John was beginning to feel annoyed. Why was she trying to daub mysterious patterns onto something that, as far as he was concerned, was singularly unremarkable? 'Perhaps she was waiting whilst her friend stopped a car,' he said.

As Harriet reached up to pull the blind on the kitchen window, she looked over in the direction of the house, now silhouetted ominously against the moonlit sky. In what she guessed must be one of the upstairs windows, there was a light moving from left to right and then back again, as if someone were walking around with an old-fashioned oil lamp.

'There's somebody in that house,' Harriet said. 'I saw a light move in one of the windows.'

This was an avenue of conversation that John was not even about to venture down. It was obvious that, give the option, Harriet would have him drive her out of this place in pitch darkness, and there was no way he was game for that. 'Come on,' he said, stepping up behind her, slipping his arms round her waist and planting a kiss on her neck, 'time for bed.'

'Bed? But it's only half past...' Harriet saw the sly grin on his face and all thoughts of the light she had seen in the house were banished to another day.

IV

IN DREAMS

Harriet had no idea what time it was when the harrowing scream cut through her slumber and woke her with a nauseating jolt. It felt as if she had only drifted off seconds beforehand. She turned her head and as her eyes adjusted to the darkness she could see the shape of John sleeping peacefully next to her. Her nightgown felt damp and was sticking to her back. Harriet lay still for a few moments, sweat beading up on her forehead as her ears strained through the sound of the heavy rain on the roof for even the vaguest indication that the scream had been something more than a product of her nightmare.

Nothing.

Their love-making had been protracted and energetic. Afterwards, with the patter of rain on the roof adding a blissful cosiness to the inside of their little home on wheels, they had snuggled down under the covers recollecting some of the more outrageous places in which they had made love in the past, giggling like mischievous children at their audacity. Eventually drowsiness had embraced them. John had slipped into untroubled repose but Harriet's had been somewhat less restful.

She had dreamed of walking amongst the trees, basking in a warm breeze that had suddenly turned fiercely cold. She became aware that she had no clothes on. As she looked around at the beautiful clothing dangling from the branches of the trees, pondering how she was going to afford such finery, the bright autumn colours of the forest melted away into frightening shadows and the two girls she had seen at the roadside appeared on either side of her. Capes billowing in the icy wind, they walked up to Harriet. She tried to cover herself, but the girls discarded their cloaks to reveal semi-translucent naked bodies and began caressing Harriet with long, gold-painted fingernails that raised goosebumps on her arms and legs. The blonde-haired girl pushed her back against a tree - a tree that was shaped like the Wolseley - and pinned her there. Harriet struggled to break free but the girl had an iron grip and the harder she tried to move the more impossible a task it seemed to be. Harriet squeezed her eyes tightly shut to make it all go away, but the blonde's mouth forced down against hers and she was aware of the other girl's dark hair brushing her thighs. Snaking hands entwined her and sharp fingernails dug painfully into her fleshy buttocks. Splayed naked across the bonnet of the Wolseley tree, she could feel the tongue between her legs, slithering from back to front across her labia, probing her vagina and flicking at her clitoris. As she surrendered herself to the overwhelming sensations of desire and began to return the kiss, so the blonde-haired girl's grip loosened. Harriet writhed in ecstasy as the silvery bark cracked and shredded beneath her. She opened her eyes and looked down at the gently rocking head. She could feel herself getting wet down below, but when the girl looked up it was not the fluid of love smeared on her lips. It was blood. Harriet's blood, which was flowing down her legs in burning rivers of lava. The faces of both girls were awash with red, each fixed in a petrifying rictus. And then that guttural scream...

Harriet reached for her watch on the bedside cabinet, but it was too dark inside the caravan to read the face. She still had an uneasy feeling in her stomach, only this time she could isolate its source. This was an irrational guilt trip. Harriet had no sexual interest in females whatsoever. She had never looked at or even thought of another woman in that way before. Okay, once perhaps, but that was years ago when she'd been at college and she had never even considered acting upon her impulses. Yet the dream had been so real. And the emotions that had boiled up within her... they were irrefutable. What's more, she liked them. She liked them a great deal in fact.

Fuck, she thought, suddenly alarmed by the extent of her arousal, *I'm getting wet just thinking about it...*

33

Beside her John was still sleeping contentedly. Moving as quietly as she could so as not to wake him, Harriet slipped her legs from beneath the blankets and got up. She filled a glass with cool water from the tap and sat down at the table, wiping away the perspiration from her forehead with her arm. Beside her, there was a small gap where the curtains didn't quite meet and, taking a sip of water, she squinted out into the blackness. She was so sure that she'd heard that scream...

The hand appeared out of nowhere and, with a sickening thud, collided with the glass just inches away from Harriet's face. Her eyes wide, she let out a piercing shriek - 'John!' - and stumbled back from the window, knocking over the six-foot fishing rod that had been left propped up against the table. The hand, streaked with something black - no, not black, red -

Is that blood??

- slipped down the glass and out of sight. Harriet was trembling uncontrollably and staring fixedly at the window as John, who'd leapt out of bed like a man on the receiving end of 20,000 volts, switched on the light.

'What on earth's the matter?' he shouted, his eyes bleary as they adjusted to the brightness.

'There's somebody outside,' Harriet panted, struggling to control her breathing. 'I saw a big hand right there on the window.'

John couldn't believe it. This was ridiculous: 'At this time of night in this weather nobody's going to be roaming around outside. You must have been dreaming. What were you doing out of bed anyway?'

Harriet was on the verge of hysteria. 'Bad dream,' she managed to say, fighting back the tears. 'Needed a glass of water.'

'You see? Just like I thought. You were dreaming.'

'No!'

Harriet was *not* going to be talked down on this one. She knew what she had seen was no dream. 'Just a minute ago I heard a scream, it woke me up. I got myself some water and

34

then suddenly this horrible hand...' Her voice trailed away. The expression on John's face spoke volumes. He was even shaking his head. It was clear that he didn't believe a word she was saying.

'Come on, darling,' he said, his voice adopting the tone of a parent patronising a child, 'let's get back to sleep.'

Harriet was almost lost for words. 'You don't honestly think I can get any sleep *now*, do you?!' They stared at each other in silence for a few moments.

There was only one way this was going to be settled. John shrugged, struggled into his heavy overcoat and pulled out a torch from the cupboard under the sink. Still shaking his head and muttering something along the lines of Harriet needing a glass of whisky, not water, he unlocked the door and stepped barefoot out into the lashing rain. His pyjama bottoms were soaked through in seconds. He flashed the torch beam back and forth in front of him, then as quickly as he could he circled the car, trying each of the doors as he went. They were securely locked. He made his way round to the far side of the caravan, feeling the wet mud seeping up between his toes. There was nothing to see. He aimed the torch in the direction of the trees, but there really wasn't much point; it was made for neither long range illumination nor penetrating heavy rain.

Using his coat sleeve to mop away the rivulets of water streaming down his face, John hurried back inside. Harriet was waiting nervously by the open door with two large fluffy bath towels. John peeled off his sodden coat and she swiftly wrapped the towels around him and began to rub vigorously.

'There's no-one out there, darling, I assure you, so relax,' John said, shivering. 'You've got to convince yourself that you were dreaming.'

Harriet managed to force a smile. She nodded. She would concede that the scream might - just *might* - have been part of her nightmare. But that hand... that had been far too real for comfort.

V

DANGEROUS LIAISONS

Drifting wisps of vapour rose from the wet grass in the vast cemetery adjacent to the Farnsworth estate as the last traces of the rainstorm were vanquished by dazzling sunlight. It shimmered through the trees and danced playfully across the myriad of crumbling gravestones. The cemetery was the sort of place over which passers-by might opine that there could surely be nowhere more peaceful in which one could wish to be laid to rest. Circled by ancient oaks, it was indeed an enchanting spot... if, that is, one could overlook its *raison d'être*.

The bell inside the tower of the tiny church that stood in one corner of the idyllic burial place sounded seven times.

Harriet opened her eyes, momentarily unsure of where she was. Then the recollections of the night flooded into her mind and she sat up. John had his back to her and was, predictably, still blissfully lost in the midst of some dream or other. Harriet pulled aside the curtain above the headboard and looked out towards the woods. How unreal the memories of a bad night always seemed once blessed daylight arrived to bleach the fearful darkness.

She blinked several times, not sure if her eyes were deceiving her. No, it wasn't her imagination. There they were. Moving through the trees, dressed in the same swarthy vestments as they had been the previous day... the two women hitchhikers. Immediately Harriet thought of her dream and she felt her stomach tighten. The women certainly weren't dawdling, she thought, in fact they were all but running. Long, purposeful strides. And then, as quickly as they had come into view, the figures dissolved into the undergrowth and were gone.

Harriet rubbed her eyes, yawned, and laid back on her pillow trying to cast the two women from her mind; it was far too early in the morning for enigmas. Five more minutes and she'd get up and prepare some breakfast. John would appreciate waking to the smell of coffee. Truth be told, even though she was in no doubt as to the events of the night, Harriet felt a shade guilty over having made John go poking around in the pouring rain. Her brow furrowed.

What on earth were those girls doing in the woods at this time of the day?

✻

A mile or two away, an ambulance pulled up at the side of the road. There was already a police car parked there and two uniformed officers were standing in the leaf-strewn gully beside an upturned car. The car looked remarkably like the one that had stopped to pick up Fran the day before-hand. The radiator grille and bonnet were severely buckled as if it had struck something at great speed; long, ragged scrape marks ran along the paintwork on one side, suggesting the car might have travelled some distance off its wheels; both the passenger and driver's doors were crumpled inwards and jammed solid. The windscreen was laterally bisected, top to bottom, by a single ugly crack, bedimmed with blotches of coagulating crimson. Pressed up against the glass on the inside was a man's face, mouth gaping to reveal two rows of smashed and bloodied teeth, eyes staring wide but seeing nothing.

The two men in the ambulance climbed down into the ditch and set about separating the corpse from its impromptu coffin.

✻

John popped the last piece of toast crust into his mouth and began plastering a second slice with a liberal serving of Robinson's thick-cut lemon marmalade. Harriet was enthusiastically demolishing a bowl full of cornflakes.

'There must be a church near here,' she was saying

between mouthfuls of the golden cereal. 'It was the chiming of the clock that woke me. Then I saw them pass by - the same two women that were on the road yesterday.'

'A coincidence,' John retorted with evident disinterest.

'Yes, but it *was* them. They were walking quickly, one behind the other.'

John simply couldn't understand why this was becoming such an obsession. He finished spreading the preserve on his toast and took a large bite out of it. Munching, he said, 'So perhaps they live somewhere close by.'

Harriet wasn't letting it go. 'But even so,' she said, 'what on earth were they doing at this hour of the morning? They didn't look normal.'

John stifled a guffaw. 'No? Well what *did* they look like then?'

'I can't explain exactly.' Harriet knew he was mocking her again. 'But they gave me a very strange feeling.'

John took another bite of his breakfast. 'Since we arrived at this spot everything seems strange to you. You see hands and ghosts just about everywhere.' *Ooops, one derogatory comment too many.*

John could see the hurt in Harriet's eyes. Finishing his toast, he brushed the crumbs from his mouth and stood up. Laid out on the floor was a collection of fishing apparatus - his rod, reels, spools of wire, an assortment of boxes containing hooks and lures - and he knelt down and began to sort through it. 'It's a beautiful morning and I'm going fishing.' He smiled. 'Catch us something tasty for supper, eh?'

And that was exactly how he passed the whole day, returning to the caravan only once to collect a ham sandwich and a can of Coca-Cola. The calmness of the lake had a hypnotic effect on him and the hours slipped away like minutes.

John had been bitten by the fishing bug just after his father had passed away prematurely when John was only ten years old. A sympathetic family friend had made a great deal of effort to keep young John from getting under his grief-stricken mother's feet, and often took him out on fishing trips. The man had quickly become a surrogate dad and their time together proved to be a consolation for John too; the solitude and long periods of introspection and reflection were an invaluable part of his own mourning process. Now there was nothing he enjoyed more than fishing, even though the amount of time he was able to devote to it these days was minimal.

Harriet, who fancied herself as something of an amateur artist - in actuality she was very good and John had told her so often - was, in spite of her ill ease, drawn to the imposing edifice of Farnsworth Hall. She spent most of the day pencilling a preliminary sketch in preparation for a painting.

By mid-afternoon the light was beginning to fade and she made her way back to the caravan where she was heartened to find John waiting for her with mugs of steaming hot chocolate.

✲

Ted Gorman's day had not gone at all as he'd planned. Waking a little after ten with a splitting headache over his right eye -

It's your own fault, Ted old boy, cheap plonk does it every time.

- the very thought of breakfast turned his stomach. So he'd rolled over and drifted back to sleep. Waking again around one-thirty and just managing to miss lunch as the dining room closed up, he narrowly avoided another inquisition from the Manager, Mr. Potter, and took a short walk to fend off the nagging remnants of his headache. It was during that walk - more specifically over a cup of tea and two stale jam donuts in the Copper Kettle Tea Rooms at the top of the road - that he'd at last come to a decision over his future with Howard & Sons. It was almost four o'clock when he finally departed the car park of The Wayfarer Inn, intent on making it home by seven. His plans were to alter dramatically.

Not ten minutes later, stopped in one of the nearby lanes,

he leant over and unlocked the passenger door. The tall, elegant woman climbed silently into the comfortable mock-leather seat and pull the door shut. She pushed aside her purple-lined cape to reveal a long black gown slit to the hip. As she settled herself back, the gap parted to expose a tantalising glimpse of pale flesh.

Ted put the car into first and pulled away, unaware of a second woman stood back among the trees. For a few seconds she watched the car leaving and then darted away.

Ted flashed the winning Gorman smile at his passenger. She had large, dark brown doe eyes and a wide, generous mouth that Ted thought would be heavenly to kiss. Her long, chestnut brown hair cascaded over slender shoulders. She returned his smile but said nothing.

'You're not the usual hitchhiker,' Ted ventured. 'No backpack. No woolly hat. No destination scribbled on a old scrap of cardboard. What's your name?'

'Fran,' the woman replied.

'Like Francis?'

'No, Francesca actually. But I prefer Fran.'

'That's a nice name,' Ted smiled. 'My name's Ted. Ted Gorman. What are you doing on the road at this time of the day?'

Fran thought for a moment, as if preparing a suitable answer as opposed to proffering anything near the truth. She said, 'I decided to take a stroll and then realised it was getting late. I don't live far from here.'

Harnessing the desire to keep staring at the woman's beautiful leg, Ted kept his eyes squarely on the road ahead. 'Well, Fran,' he said, 'you should be careful accepting lifts from strange men.'

'Are *you* strange?' Fran purred, raising her eyebrows.

'Strangers I mean. It could be dangerous.'

'And are *you* dangerous, Mr. Gorman?' Now she was teasing him.

'Ted. Please call me Ted. Let's just say that I've had my moments.' He winked.

'Hmmmmmm.' Fran smiled and slid the tip of her tongue

across her top lip in a gesture of mock sexual promiscuity. 'Lucky me.'

Ted glanced at her and for the merest instant he would have sworn that there was a deep yellow glow in her eyes. But if it really had been there it vanished as quickly as it had appeared.

Imagining things. Must have been the lights from the dashboard...

In every sense Ted found her beguiling. 'And what about you then?', he smiled. 'Are you, er... receptive to dangerous men?'

'Let's just say that I've had my moments.'

Keeping one hand on the wheel, Ted pulled out a cigarette and, placing it between his lips, offered the packet to Fran. She shook her head. Ted thought better of it, slipped the cigarette back into the carton and tossed it into the glove compartment. The lightweight small-talk, garnished with benign innuendo, continued for a few minutes until they neared the turning off onto the Farnsworth estate.

Ted was just saying, 'You remind me very much of someone I knew a long time ago,' when Fran pointed to a gap in the trees ahead and interrupted him.

'Slow down, we're almost there. It's the next on the left.'

Ted complied and guided the BMW smoothly through the turn onto the track leading out to the lake. Narrow wasn't the word for it. As the car crawled slowly through the mud and leaves, Ted looked at Fran. 'Are you sure that this track is meant for a car?' he asked doubtfully.

Fran's response provided him with precious little peace of mind: 'It's a shortcut. It's not often used.'

'Hmm, I gathered as much.'

In spite of Ted's concern that he'd end up firmly wedged in the mud, the BMW exited the far end of the track. Ted pressed down on the pedal and they sped across the wide expanse of grass and onto the forecourt of Farnsworth Hall.

'I trust I can tempt you to come inside for a drink?' Fran said as they cruised to a halt.

Harriet was just washing off the dishes when she heard

the sound of the car pass nearby. John had enjoyed his day by the lake but it had proven less than productive in the comestibles department. Harriet had consoled him by grilling up two of the delicious steaks she'd bought for the freezer when they'd stopped for lunch in Godalming the previous day.

She peered out of the kitchen window through the dusk towards the house and watched Ted climb from the driver's side. Then the passenger side door opened.

'Hey, John, look. It's one of those women with a man.'

John looked up from his book. This was becoming *really* tiresome. 'Oh, again?!' he grumbled.

Harriet beckoned him over. 'Look, there's his car if you need convincing.'

John stepped up beside her and looked out at the BMW. 'I don't need convincing for God's sake. I just don't see anything peculiar about it, that's all.' He put his arm round Harriet's shoulders and gave her a loving squeeze. 'Come on,' he said. 'You go and sit down, I'll finish up here.'

As John set his mind to the mundane task of washing crockery and Harriet perused the selection of cheap and cheerful romantic paperback novels that lined one shelf of the bedside cabinet - she selected one entitled "Meet Me in Istanbul", with a cover artwork of a young couple embracing in front of the St. Sophia Mosque - Fran was leading Ted around the side of Farnsworth Hall. If it weren't for Ted, the walk would have been marked by silence.

'Are you English?' he asked Fran. 'You don't look it.'

Fran didn't answer but instead cast him a rather disdainful look.

'Well?' he pressed.

'If I told you you wouldn't believe me,' she replied.

What kind of half-arsed answer is that?

They arrived in front of a large wooden door with brass fittings. It wasn't locked, which Ted fleetingly thought rather odd, but nonetheless he followed Fran inside. As his eyes became accustomed to the dark, he could see they were standing in an unfurnished hallway that looked sorely in need of redecoration. Fran was a few feet away from him at the foot of a wide staircase that curved upwards out of sight into blackness.

'Does this kind of thing excite you?' she smiled provocatively. Her voice, her manner, her body... everything about her was utterly intoxicating.

Ted had to admit to himself that regardless of his curiosity, this whole set-up was beginning to bother him slightly. 'Sometimes,' he said. 'Why?'

Again the teasing expression. 'Now, now, don't be too impatient.' She began to climb the stairs. 'Come.'

They walked unhurriedly up to the first floor and Ted saw that they were at the end of a long hallway. Once again furnishings were conspicuous by their absence and the stale scent of rooms long denied a whiff of fresh air nipped at Ted's nostrils. They walked without talking down the hall and through a door at the end. Before them was another flight of steps. Ted tutted aloud. Fran stopped and turned to face him. 'I get the impression that you're not too keen on this kind of expedition,' she said. 'Don't worry.'

Don't worry?!

This whole caper was beginning to seem ill-conceived. Ted was thinking that maybe he ought to just walk out of here, get into his car and drive away. 'Now look here,' he began, 'I find you very attractive but this stroll is becoming rather boring. What the hell is all this about?' His tone was becoming angrier by the moment. 'You can't tell me that you use this dump for your dates.'

Fran's retort was equally indignant. 'Certainly not!' The annoyance vanished, supplanted by a matter of factness. 'Where we're going is quite different from all this.' She waved a hand in the air. 'And it's too late to go back now.' Fran saw the expression on Ted's face. She added quickly, 'I mean it would be a shame to retrace our steps after having come so far. And we are nearly there.' The tone became coaxing. 'It'll be worth the exertion... I promise.'

The craving that this beautiful creature provoked in Ted welled up and quashed his ire. 'Well...' he sought for something apt to dissipate the growing tension, '...I hope you have a map I can use to find my way back out again.' That seemed to do the trick. The corners of Fran's mouth curled into a half-smile.

Little head doing the thinking for the big head... as usual, Ted old boy.

They made their way to the top of the second staircase and into another lengthy corridor, this one lined on either side by four or five doors. Fran opened the first one to the left and Ted followed her inside.

VI

AFTER DARK

The draughtiness aside, the room in which Ted found himself standing was like nothing the other parts of the house he had thus far seen could have prepared him for. The experience was tantamount to stepping from a pigsty into a palace.

There was no prevailing theme to the predominantly cinnamon decor, rather a surprisingly aesthetic blend of furnishings and artefacts from across the continents. The unobtrusive wallpaper, dappled with tiny daisies which only became apparent if one stood up close, was offset by a number of framed church brass rubbings and cross-stitch hangings. Beneath each of the hangings, back to the wall, there was an upright armchair upholstered in chocolate brown velveteen. All around the room there were ornaments large and small, from a pair of life-size sculpted figures of Indian boys to scaled-down carved ivory lions set atop ornate stone plinths. A pair of large, green-shaded lamps, each sat upon a well-polished hexagonal wooden table with intricate rococo panelling, provided most of the subtle illumination. A cafe-au-lait carpet of the deepest pile stretched from wall to wall and there were several zebra skin rugs - almost certainly reproduction, Ted thought - laid out at angles to the centrepiece, which was a luxurious chocolate brown lounge settee around which were laying a number of outsize scatter cushions.

Against one wall was a long, open-fronted glass display case, laden mostly with bottles and vases in a variety of shapes and patterns. On the opposite side of the room there was an open fireplace, the wrought iron grate of which was decorated with Oriental-style dragons. The focal point on the white marble mantel was an expensive-looking clock - which Ted observed wasn't functioning - flanked by dainty jade figurines of angels. A heady aroma of jasmine permeated the cool air.

Ted had never been in a room quite like it before in his life, and he couldn't imagine that he was ever likely to be again.

Fran was standing beside the settee, watching him, apparently unmoved by his surprise. 'This is my place,' she said. 'Do you like it?'

Ted nodded. 'Well, it's better than the rest of the house.' He looked around him again. 'I can't believe it. Does it all belong to you?'

'I'm only a guest.'

Any worries that Ted might have had were melting away amid the grandeur of this exceptional chamber. 'What other surprises have you got for me?' he asked.

'We'll see,' Fran said. A thin smile appeared on her lips and she crossed the room. In the far corner was another door which up until now Ted hadn't noticed; framed on either side by exotic ferns in tall, black free-standing vases trimmed with gold, it was partially hidden by a wicker screen. 'Now be a darling and light the fire while I get us something to drink. Then make yourself comfortable.' She paused in the doorway. 'Relax. The worst's over.'

Fran left the room and Ted was alone. He went over to the open fireplace which had already been prepared with kindling and ample firewood. Kneeling at the hearth, he withdrew the Ronson from his pocket. The flint sparked but the lighter failed to ignite.

Now that's a first.

He tried again. Twice more. No luck.

Bloody hell, I only refilled it last week.

Ted angrily stuffed the lighter back in his pocket, stood up and looked around. His eyes fell upon a packet of Swan Vestas on the mantelpiece. He reached them down, struck one and shortly the flames were licking at the air, discharging the devil's breath into the room. Ted squatted in front of the fire, rubbing his hands together, revelling in the warmth. He stood up and walked over to the display case to scrutinise some of the trinkets on show. At one end, mounted on the wall, was a frame about two feet square and several inches deep that housed a number of pinned butterflies. The most attractive was a large and very beautiful death's-head moth, so named for the markings on its upper thorax which resemble a human skull. Ted stared at it. He looked at the small assembly of ammonites encased in chunks of rock and remembered picking around for fossils at the foot of the cliffs in Devon when he was a child.

What caught his eye next, startling him somewhat, was not the array of probably very valuable glassware on the display case. Laid between two tall-necked blue glass vases bearing a hand-painted Oriental design, was a knife. A particularly vicious-looking huntsman's knife, with an elegant carved wooden grip and a ten-inch curved steel blade. Ted frowned. Had it been part of a collection, given the diverse nature of the curios in the room, it wouldn't have been out of place. But as a solitary whisper of latent violence amidst the otherwise relatively innocuous ornamentation, it projected a most disturbing aura.

The door opened and Fran reappeared carrying a tray upon which was an open bottle of Mouton Rothschild and two silver goblets. She had removed her cloak to reveal an extremely becoming, figure-hugging black silk gown with silver bootlace cords across each shoulder. The clinging nature of the gown made it abundantly evident that she had on no underwear.

Fran set down the tray on a low table at one end of the settee and walked over to an old, dusty-looking gramophone. She selected an LP from the small selection stacked beside it, placed it on the turntable, and the sweet, evocative melancholy of Pyotr Ilyich Tchaikovsky's "Scène from Swan Lake" filled the room. It was one of Ted's favourite classical pieces. Fran kicked off her heels, and made herself comfortable on the cushions. Ted perched himself on the edge of the settee and filled each of the goblets to the brim. He passed one to Fran, admiring as he did so her voluminous bosom which was threatening to burst from the confines of the low-cut gown.

'I was asking myself...' Ted began. There was so much he wanted to know about this ravishing woman that he wasn't sure where to begin.

Fran had the goblet to her lips. 'Asking?'

'Well,' Ted continued, 'I don't expect that you should divulge all your secrets, but...'

'Go on,' Fran urged him, 'just ask.'

'Is there a limit to the questions?'

Fran took a sip of the crimson nectar. 'There's a limit to the answers.'

Ted settled himself back and took a large mouthful of wine. Fran sat patiently waiting to be interrogated.

Okay, let's begin with something basic.

'Do you live here alone?' Ted asked.

There was no hesitation, though the response was somewhat ambiguous. 'I often receive guests.'

I bet you do, you temptress. How many times have you played out this little scenario?... And with how many men?

'What do you do for a living?'

Fran looked thoughtful. 'I'm searching all the time. Searching for interesting people.' Once again, fairly non-specific.

'Well,' Ted paused. 'Do you find *me* interesting?'

Fran raised an eyebrow and smiled. 'If I didn't think you had potential, my dear, you wouldn't be here.'

Ted swallowed another draught of the wine and glanced at the label on the bottle. It was the 1955, quite excellent. 'It's difficult to find really interesting people,' he said.

'I know,' Fran replied, 'but I keep searching. I know how to fend for myself.' She raised her goblet and made a circular motion in the air. 'I feel happier here than anywhere else. These walls have become my friends, my confidantes.'

Ted listened to her intently, watching the oh-so-desirable lips forming each word. He longed to kiss them. And yet, deeply attracted to her as he was, every fibre in his being was screaming at him that something here just wasn't quite right. Danger. Get out now. *Danger!*

He allowed the pleasant effect that the claret was having on him to wash over the rationale. 'You're not so easy to understand, Fran,' he said, draining his goblet and promptly refilling it.

'That's the way I have to be accepted,' she said, 'with no questions and no explanations.'

Ted grinned. 'However you wish, sweet lady. In any event, I think this turned out to be my lucky day.'

'Don't *ever* say that!' Fran set down her goblet on the tray. A baleful look appeared in her eyes.

'Oh, I don't really mind unusual situations,' Ted continued. 'They come on their own. They're the spice that makes life interesting. Exciting even. Like us meeting on the road today.' Now it was Fran hanging on Ted's every word, her lips slightly parted, her eyes searching for... for what? The moment was perfect. Ted put down his goblet and leant towards her. She turned up her face to receive him and their mouths met in a long, impassioned kiss.

Lips still pressed firmly together, they manoeuvred themselves until Fran was laid back on the cushions with Ted's full weight upon her. With one hand he explored her curves, working his way up her body and slipping the silver cords from her each shoulder.

Suddenly Fran pulled her mouth away from his. 'Wait!' Ted sat back looking a little puzzled as Fran stood up, picked up the half-full bottle of wine and walked to the door. 'Not here. Come.'

Ted got to his feet and followed her. They crossed the hallway and went into the room opposite. It was a bedroom. The decor here was far more simplistic, at least compared to the opulence of the room they had just left. The floorboards were bare, though polished, and the plainness of the white walls was broken up at intervals by a series of old framed prints depicting erotic images of a bygone era. Heavy red velvet curtains embroidered with silver thread hung over the windows. It occurred to Ted that there was something familiar about the room, but he couldn't quite pinpoint what.

Shaking off the feeling *déjà vu*, he watched as Fran crossed to the bed. She set down the bottle of Mouton Rothschild and unzipped her gown, allowing it to drop to the floor around her ankles. Ted had been right; she had on no underwear.

'Your hair is very beautiful,' he observed as he watched Fran run her hands through the mane of silky chestnut tresses. She turned into the light to reveal a thatch of downy pubic curls foresting the tantalising V at the top of her thighs. 'And it's rewarding to see that the collars and cuffs match,' he chuckled, rather pleased with his small witticism. Fran smiled, but the full lips held no humour.

In the dim lamplight her naked form adopted a mesmerising iridescence. She had one of the most magnificent bodies that Ted had ever been fortunate enough to set eyes on. He felt himself getting hard. As he quickly shed his own clothes, Fran sat down on the edge of the bed and emptied the last of the wine into two crystal flutes that were sitting on the bedside table. By the time she was finished, Ted had climbed in under the covers and was leaning back casually against the headboard admiring her nakedness. The expression on his face was that of the cat about to get the cream.

As Fran put down the bottle, Ted was suddenly aware of a faint scuffling noise coming from the passageway outside. He looked past her to the door, half expecting it to open. It didn't. He said, 'Are you sure we're alone, Fran?'

'What makes you ask?' she replied, apparently oblivious to the sound - which had now stopped.

Odd, she must have heard it.

'I get the strong feeling we're not.' Ted said suspiciously.

Fran's response was about as distracting as distractions can be. She swung her legs up onto the bed, spread them wide until she was straddling Ted, and planted a foot down on either side of his head so that he was staring directly into her crotch, no more than twelve inches from his face. As he opened his mouth to speak, Fran moistened the tip of her index finger with claret, reached down between her legs and,

50

without taking her eyes off his, traced it lightly across the lips of her sex. Then she felt for Ted's hand and guided his fingers to her. She raised an eyebrow: 'You were saying...?'

Her body was scented with perfume; Ted recognised it as Le Bleu. Unable to control himself, with an animal grunt he lurched forward and buried his head between her thighs, his mouth working crazily. Fran's hands grabbed him roughly by the hair, pulling him hard to her and grinding against his face. Ted sprinkled a trail of kisses across her torso, grabbing hungrily at her full breasts and biting down hard on each of the nipples; Fran breathed in sharply through clenched teeth - as much from pain as pleasure. As Ted's mouth crushed greedily against hers she spread herself as wide as she could. Reaching down between his legs, she gripped his rigid penis and guided him inside.

Breathlessly, she said, 'Fuck me. Fuck me hard!'

Who was Ted Gorman to deny this beautiful lady so simple a request? He plunged into her and began to thrash in and out, in and out, faster and faster as he felt himself building to a peak.

Not yet, too soon...

Ted slowed his pace to control the urge to explode and carefully withdrew. 'Christ...' Breathing hard he rolled back onto the covers.

'Don't stop!' Fran got to her knees and reverse straddled his hips so that her back was to him; Ted found himself gazing at the flawless curves of her buttocks. He reached for them, at the same time feeling her cool fingers encircle his shaft. In a moment he was inside her again. Ted grabbed Fran's hips as she began to slide up and down, and he watched her buttocks rise and fall... rise and fall.... rise and fall. Sitting upright and gnawing at the soft flesh on her shoulders, he reached around from behind and roughly pawed her breasts, pulling, scratching. The muscles in her vagina contracted and relaxed expertly in time with her movements until Ted could prolong the moment not a second longer. With a gasp of euphoria, and Fran's cries of pleasure vibrating in his ears, he filled her.

In the early hours of the morning - which, for no particular reason, Ted later thought must have been sometime
between two and three - the sound of running feet echoed
through the corridors of Farnsworth Hall.

Ted opened his eyes. For a man who'd just had the best
sex of his life, he didn't look at all well. His face was pasty
and glistened with a sheen of sweat, his eyes were dark-
ringed and bloodshot. Barely awake, his lolled head to one
side and he looked at Fran. What he saw was quite
disarming. She was staring at him, her body motionless -

Christ, is she dead?

- no, not quite motionless. She was breathing. Yet the eyes
continued to stare directly at him, unblinking. With some
effort Ted lifted his hand, which felt like a lead weight, and
moved it about in front of her face. 'Fran?' There was no
reaction. The eyes maintained their steady gaze. She was
asleep. Asleep, but with her eyes open.

That's fucking spooky!

Again there was a movement in the hallway outside the
room and the door began to open. As Ted watched, hardly
able to hold up his head, it swung inwards about a third of
the way and stopped. He tried to get out of bed, but the
effort required to do so was almost beyond him. He felt
terrible.

Didn't drink all that much... this is ridiculous.

He managed to slide onto the floor and then pulled
himself to his feet with the aid of the bedstead. Heedless of
his nakedness, he attempted to focus on the partially-open
door, expecting at any moment to see someone appear out of
the shadows. But his vision was blurry and he was having
trouble just keeping his eyes open, never mind remaining on
his feet. Shivering as if in the grip of a fever, he let go of the
bedpost and staggered the few short paces to the door,
almost lost his balance and fell heavily against it. With a loud
bang it slammed shut.

Ted paused for a moment to regain his balance and

looked over towards the bed. With her back to him, the nude, curvaceous form of Fran slept on undisturbed. Using all the strength he could muster, he crawled on all fours across the room and hoisted his aching limbs up onto the bed, collapsing face-down into the pillows.

VII

DAYLIGHT

When Ted opened his eyes again it was morning. A thin
shaft of light peeked through the curtains and sliced across
the floorboards. The bed beside him was empty.

The first thing to pass through his mind as he lay staring
up at the ceiling was the mysterious incident of the early
hours. Had someone opened the door? Maybe, but it was
shut now. Of course it was; he had shut it. Had Fran really
been staring at him like a corpse? Possibly. Or maybe it had
all been a dream.

No, not all of it.

Although Ted felt a little less of the frightening ague that
had all but disabled him when he tried - or at least *thought* he
had tried - to get out of bed, considering he'd had a full
night's sleep he didn't feel particularly refreshed. In fact he
felt unnaturally fatigued.

Ted sat up and looked around the room. Fran's gown was
gone but his own clothes were still strewn across the floor
where he'd left them. Wearily, he climbed off the bed and,
yawning intermittently, got dressed. It was only when he
came to put on his shirt that he felt the pain in his left arm.
He looked down and his eyes widened -

What in damnation?.....

- at the sight of an obscene gash, four-inches long at least, on
the inside of his elbow. There wasn't as much blood in
evidence as he would have expected from such a severe
wound, but it nevertheless gaped open and was weeping a
little. It looked very deep. Now the pain began to pulse
through his arm - how hadn't he felt it before? - and a wave
of nausea engulfed him. He managed to pull on his shirt and
do up the buttons, but he left the cuffs on the sleeves open.

Thinking over the events of the previous evening, trying
to fathom out how and when he could have cut himself so

badly, Ted walked across to the curtains, pulled one aside and looked out. From here he could only see part of a walled terrace and the overgrown gardens at the back of the house sloping down to the woods. He bent to pick up his jacket and felt for his pigskin wallet on the inside pocket; a cursory check confirmed that nothing was missing.

As he put on his wristwatch, tutting to himself as he saw that it had stopped at 3.43, he noticed the crystal flutes on the small table on Fran's side of the bed. They were broken. One particularly jagged-looking shard was smeared with red. Ted could feel the bile rising in his throat. He choked it back and pulled back the blankets on the bed. There, where he had slept, was a large, dark patch of blood. It was still wet.

With his jacket hanging from one shoulder - out of necessity of comfort rather than for the rakish effect it had - Ted walked out of the bedroom and crossed the corridor. The sitting room was, unsurprisingly, as deserted as the rest of the house now appeared to be. Using one of the Swan Vestas to light a cigarette, he stuck them in his pocket and made his way down the hallway, trying each of the doors as he went. Most were locked, those that weren't yielded little of interest. As he reached the end of the hall, a scuffling noise sounded from the direction of the staircase. Ted spun around.

'Hey! Who's there?' There was no reply. As quickly as his tired bones would carry him, he hurried back down the hall to the top of the stairwell. 'Fran? *Fran?!!*' Silence.

Ted slowly made his way downstairs and found himself idly counting the steps as he went. He reached the bottom at thirty-nine and smiled to himself; John Buchan would have been well at home here. 'Fran!' he shouted again. This was getting ridiculous.

He went back upstairs and into the living room, mumbling under his breath, 'Where the bloody hell do people go here in the mornings?' He pulled back the curtain from the window which looked out over the grounds to the front of the house. There was nothing of note to see other than the car and caravan parked off to the right by the edge of the trees. The door at the back was open but there was no sign of activity. As he let the curtain fall, a searing pain ran through the length of his arm and blood seeped through the sleeve of his white cotton shirt. He had to get some medical attention, and quickly.

Ted walked back across the room, but as he passed the display case, something caught his eye that made him stop. Between the two vases where the knife had been there was now only a space. The knife was laying on the table at the end of the settee. There was blood on the blade.

Right! That's it. I'm getting out of here.

By the time Ted reached the back door, he had regained some of his strength. Two or three deep gulps of the cold morning air sharpened his wits further still; hurrying round the side of the house, he was back at his car in less than a minute.

Steering wasn't a problem, but shifting gears sent agonising waves of pain coursing up and down Ted's injured arm. More blood oozed out onto his sleeve, which was beginning to look like a sorely abused piece of blotting paper. As he set off towards the trees, he again spotted the caravan. Help just might be closer at hand than seeking out a doctor. Ted turned the wheel and the car bumped its way over the rough stretch of grass towards the caravan.

John was in the middle of preparing a flask of coffee to take out fishing with him, and Harriet had just finished cleaning her paint brushes in white spirit - she'd been too lazy to do it the night before, and at least one of them was now ruined - when Ted appeared in the open doorway. Harriet jumped.

'Sorry to startle you. I hope you'll excuse me for intruding but I've hurt myself.' Ted suddenly felt faint.

John saw him sway and took his arm. 'No problem. Come on in.'

He guided Ted to a seat and Harriet reached over - 'Just one moment.'- and scooped her brushes off the table. She moved back out of the way into the kitchen area.

Ted sat down, pulled out a handkerchief and mopped the sweat from his brow. Regaining his composure, he said, 'It's nothing serious. Only a little cut really, but it hurts quite a bit.'

John had eased Ted's sleeve up and was inspecting the wound, which now looked quite messy. 'I'm not so sure,' he said, 'that's quite a deep cut.'

Ted forced a little chuckle. 'Did it on a piece of glass.' He saw the questioning look on John's face. 'Well, I must have had a few too many last night and fallen over on some broken glass.'

'It's pretty swollen,' John observed.

Harriet appeared beside them and set down a compact first aid kit on the table, along with a small bowl of diluted Dettol. 'Let me disinfect it,' she said.

As she touched the soaked cotton wool ball to the gash, Ted flinched and drew his arm away. Harriet apologised. 'It's alright,' Ted smiled. 'Please carry on.'

John watched Harriet cleaning away the congealed blood. 'It might hurt but it helps,' he proffered.

'Thanks for *your* help,' Ted replied. 'I don't know how far I'd have had to go to find a doctor round here. You've saved me a great deal of trouble.'

John shook his head. 'That's alright, don't mention it.'

'No, really, I mean it,' Ted said. 'With my arm in this state I couldn't have driven very far.'

'You know, you ought to rest for a while,' Harriet suggested, but Ted shook his head. 'Why not stay with us and have a cup of coffee?' she added.

'She's right, you know,' John chipped in. 'A hot cup of coffee will do you the world of good.'

The thought of a cup of coffee suddenly sounded like an inviting proposition. 'Well,' Ted said, 'that's most kind of you. Thank you very much.'

Harriet finished taping a thick square wad of gauze over the wound, got up and pulled a mug out of the cupboard. She filled it with steaming, sweet black coffee from John's flask.

'By the way, I'm John. John Bailey. And this is my wife Harriet. We're on holiday.'

Ted smiled, 'My name's Ted. You picked a fine spot for camping.'

'I don't think Harriet would agree with you,' John grinned. 'But I like it.'

Ted said, 'Have you got the correct time please?' John glanced at his watch and said that it was a little after 10.15. Ted frowned. 'It's ridiculous, but my watch has stopped,' he said. 'It's never done it before.'

✻

Not so very far away, another man's watch had stopped. It was a Rolex and its state of failure was not coincidental; it had been smashed. The man upon whose wrist the ruined timepiece was strapped was dead, a blood-sodden corpse in the process of being wrapped up on a stretcher by two ambulance men. A police car was parked nearby and another car, a red Mini Minor, sat askew, crushed up against a broad oak tree. The umpteenth fatal accident on this stretch of road in the past month. It was hardly a hot spot either, or at least it hadn't been until recently. Always the drivers had been drinking. And always such carnage resulted.

Two uniformed police officers were standing off to one side, their heads bowed, talking in hushed tones. 'Bloody awful business this,' one of them was saying.

'Too damned right,' his colleague nodded. 'Here, you know what I overheard the Guv saying to Sarge last week after that Cortina got smashed up? Only that if this spate of accidents doesn't stop he'll have to consider setting up some sort of rota for a permanent watch down here. And this is the second one since then.'

The first officer looked aghast. 'Awwww, shit, Alan!' he exclaimed. 'We're short staffed enough as it is, what with Frank retiring early. How the hell do they think they're gonna swing that one? Compulsory overtime? Hell's teeth, I can see my leave getting cancelled. Please tell me you're having me on.'

'I kid you not, that's what I heard. And that's not all

either. There's talk circulating at the station that there's more to these so-called accidents than meets the eye. I tell ya, I'm inclined to agree. I mean, let's face it, how many smashes have we had to mop up after on this bit of road in the past month? Five? Six maybe? Christ alive, Dave, there haven't been that many fatalities in a 50-mile radius of here in the past three years, never mind in a single fuckin' month! It's hardly surprising that questions are being asked in the upper echelon. Anyway, seems that the official report from the morgue on the last one was pretty much conclusive. In a nutshell there's no way that the body lost as much blood as it did at the site of the crash. Which can mean only one thing - the bugger was dead before...' He trailed off and coughed purposefully to draw his friend's attention to the approaching ambulance driver.

The man was fastening his overcoat. 'Okay lads,' he said with an inappropriate note of cheer. 'He's all parcelled up with a bow, we're on our way.'

The policeman named Dave grimaced. 'Heartless bastard. Show a little fuckin' respect.'

A couple of minutes later the ambulance pulled away and a tow truck appeared from around the bend. One of the policemen raised a hand of acknowledgement to the man behind the wheel, whose face had become regrettably familiar these past weeks.

☼

As the truck driver was busily lashing a chain to the bumper of the Mini, so Ted was finishing his coffee and feeling greatly improved for it. 'I'd best be on my way then,' he said. 'Many thanks for the coffee. And your help.'

Harriet and John both smiled. 'Think nothing of it,' John said.

Ted shook hands with the pair of them and walked to the door. John noticed that Harriet was biting her lip. As Ted stepped outside, she suddenly blurted out, 'Does anyone live in that house?'

John rolled his eyes. Ted paused on the step. 'That's a question I asked myself earlier,' he said. 'And I still haven't found an answer. Goodbye.'

They bid their visitor farewell and, as Ted walked back to his car, John gave Harriet a gentle dig in the ribs with his elbow. 'The urge was too strong, wasn't it, Miss Nosy? You had to ask him or you would have exploded.'

Harriet laughed. 'Yes, but he didn't answer my question, did he? And what about the woman we saw him with? Where's she? Why couldn't she have helped him?' John gave a non-committal grunt. Offering Harriet a cigarette, he lit one for himself and went to make a fresh flask of coffee. Harriet stayed in the doorway watching Ted's car. She expected him to drive off down the mud track to the road, but instead he was headed back in the direction of Farnsworth Hall.

'Right,' John said, screwing the top tightly onto his flask. 'I'm goin' fishing.'

'Look,' Harriet said, sounding slightly mystified. 'He's going back to the house.'

John followed her gaze, though he had no idea why. He couldn't have cared less if he tried. 'Yeah, I can see.' Grinning, he added, 'He's going back to the house,' with just enough sarcasm to imply that this turn of events, unpredictable as it might have been, was anything but mysterious.

VIII

A TIME TO KILL

Darkness came quickly.

Neither the low rumble of thunder nor the double lighting flash that followed a few moments afterwards roused Ted from his sleep.

After he'd left John and Harriet he'd parked outside the house, determined to sit it out until Fran returned. He wanted to know how his arm had been cut - if it was indeed an accident, it was one of which he had no recollection whatsoever - and where she had disappeared to. Unless she was hiding for some ridiculous reason, it didn't seem as if she was inside the house and he had no idea where she might be or how long he would have to wait. In any event, he wanted an explanation. And, if he was going to be completely honest with himself, he was hoping for a second helping of the delights served up to him the night before. Drowsiness had quickly taken hold of him and he had lost the remainder of the day in a deep, dreamless slumber.

What eventually brought Ted back into the land of the living was the sound of an approaching car. His breath, as he'd slept, had misted the inside of the windscreen. He felt for the old piece of rag that he kept stuffed down the side of his seat and wiped away the condensation from the glass. Shrugging off the stiffness in his shoulders, he rubbed his eyes and squinted as the car pulled up nose to nose with his own, its headlights shining directly into his face. There was the sound of a door slamming and something briefly broke the dazzling glare. As Ted wound down his window and leant out, Fran stepped up alongside the car and bent her face down so that it was inches away from his. There didn't seem to be any sign of surprise on her part that he was here waiting for her. 'I'm sorry about this morning,' she began, looking apologetically into his eyes. 'I had to get up at the

61

crack of dawn. I didn't like to wake you, you seemed so peaceful. I couldn't get back any earlier, I had so much to do. Will you please forgive me?'

Ted caught the scent of Le Bleu and his ire eased. He did feel annoyed, but... 'Not to worry, you're here now.' He looked past Fran. There were two figures standing, one on either side of the other car, but he couldn't make them out through the glare of the headlamps.

Fran saw him looking. 'Oh, I almost forgot,' she said. 'I'm with friends. I'm sure you'll like them.' The figure on the driver's side leant into the car and the lights went out. As Ted climbed out of the BMW a man and a woman walked over and stood beside Fran. 'This is Miriam,' Fran said, 'and her friend, Rupert.' The woman was very pretty with doll-like features and straight blonde hair. Ted noticed that she was dressed similarly to Fran, except that the cape was lined in red. The man was of stocky build and had mousey hair that was fashionably cut to shoulder length. He was clean shaven and even in the poor light Ted could see that he had one of those faces that probably only required shaving every other day. It occurred to Ted that Rupert epitomised the expression boyish good looks. In spite of his rather cheap looking houndstooth suit, Ted took an immediate liking to him.

The man extended a hand to Ted. 'Hi, Rupert Gower, pleased to meet you.'

Perfunctory greetings were exchanged. With the formalities over, the quartet made their way into the house, following the same dingy route that Ted and Fran had taken the previous night. Ted noticed that Rupert looked nervous; he smiled to himself, recalling his own uncertainty of 24 hours ago.

If this little Miriam girl is half as good in the sack as Fran, you've got the night of your life ahead of you, Rupert old son.

They reached the sitting room and Miriam went over and switched on the lights.

'It's freezing in here,' Fran said, giving a small shiver.

Ted felt in his pocket for the matches. 'I'll have the fire

alight in a jiffy,' he said. Whilst he set about doing so, and Fran went to get some refreshments, Miriam removed her cloak to reveal a beautiful scarlet gown with gold spangles that shimmered as she moved. She joined Rupert beside the display unit where he was absent-mindedly looking at the knife; had Ted noticed he might have queried how, if the house had been empty all day, it had got from the table to the display case and who had wiped away the traces of blood from the blade. But he didn't notice.

'Do you like that?' Miriam was saying, reaching out and caressing the carved haft in a blatantly carnal manner.

Rupert wasn't really listening. His mind appeared to be elsewhere. 'Look,' he said, 'may I make a phone call?'

Miriam looked regretful. 'I'm afraid not. There's no telephone in the house.'

'Oh, well,' Rupert gave a small shrug, 'it doesn't matter. It's just that I've arranged to meet some friends of mine. I would have liked to have let them know I was going to be a bit late.'

'Oh, I feel so guilty,' Miriam said, not actually sounding the least bit as if she really did.

Rupert smiled. 'It's okay.'

Ted had finished lighting the fire and it was roaring away merrily in the grate. Fran reappeared with a bottle of wine - again it was the '55 Mouton - and four goblets.

'Can I give you a hand, darling?' Miriam offered. Fran said that it wasn't necessary. They sat round in a circle, Ted on the settee with Fran, Rupert and Miriam on the floor cushions. Ted played mother, passing a filled goblet to each of them.

'I'm afraid red wine is all we've got,' Fran said, as if an apology were necessary. 'But it's a very good vintage.'

Ted raised his goblet. 'Good health,' he said.

They all tasted the wine. It was, of course, superb. Fran said to Rupert, 'Do you like it? Everyone seems to.' Rupert nodded and accepted a refill from Ted.

'The cellars here are stacked high with the stuff,' Miriam said. 'Some of it is years old.'

They chatted among themselves for a few minutes, during which time Ted managed to ascertain that Rupert was a production manager with a London-based pharmaceuticals corporation. He learned precisely nothing about Miriam, who chatted freely on most subjects, yet revealed naught about herself.

The bottle was quickly depleted. Fran picked up the empty and waggled it in the air. 'Miriam, darling, I'm afraid you'll have to go down to the cellar to fetch some more. I'm sure Rupert will be able to help you in the choice of an excellent vintage.'

'Yes, with pleasure,' Rupert said, getting to his feet.

Neither Ted nor Rupert noticed the look that passed between the two women.

'Let's go then,' Miriam said. Rupert eagerly followed her to the door like the loyal hound in pursuit of a tasty treat. Ted waited for them to leave before he spoke his mind: 'I waited for you all day until I fell asleep in the car.'

Fran gave him a sincere look of apology. 'Forgive me about this morning. I really did think I'd be back earlier.'

'This girl,' Ted said, 'your friend Miriam. Was she here last night?'

Fran shook her head. 'No, I told you, we were alone. Just you,' - she leaned over and kissed him on the nose - 'and I.'

'Does she live here with you then?' Ted pressed.

'More or less. She's my girlfriend. We have a lot in common and we get on very well together.'

'When you say she's your girlfriend...'

Fran raised an eyebrow, a mannerism that Ted was beginning to find most endearing. 'In all respects,' she said. 'Is that a problem for you?'

'No, not in the least,' Ted shook his head. 'Live and let live, I say. But it's crazy to reside in an old house like this. I heard Miriam saying that there's no telephone, and the place is almost in ruins. These walls could fall in on you at any moment.' It was something of an overstatement and Ted knew it. He promptly changed tack. 'Who is this chap Rupert?'

'A very nice man,' Fran smiled benignly.

'And how long have you known *him*?'

Ted's inquisition was becoming boring. 'Since this afternoon,' Fran said. 'He gave us a lift here.' She quickly stifled any further questions with a lingering kiss, her hand snaking down and stroking across the fly on his trousers.

✻

Harriet was unable to settle. She'd tried reading her book but couldn't concentrate, and a mug of hot chocolate - which usually soothed her nerves - had failed to weave its magic. Paranoia was brewing. She sat looking out of the window at the teeming rain, picking out specific droplets on the glass and following their journey from top to bottom until they disappeared. John was reading. If Harriet wanted to obsess over the house and its occupants then she could damned well get on with it. He'd said his piece.

'I still think we've chosen a bad spot for camping,' Harriet mused.

John didn't look up. 'I really don't see why,' he said. 'It's attractive and quiet and nobody's bothered us.'

'That's not the point. How often do you read of horrible things happening in just such a situation. A quiet, isolated corner. A couple just like us.'

John laughed. 'A couple just like *us*? Please, darling, don't start all that again.' It seemed he was being drawn back into this stupid discussion whether he liked it or not.

Harriet went on, 'First there were those two women. Then that man with the cut on his arm.'

Putting down his book, John said, 'Now you're exaggerating. The poor man came in search of help, which is perfectly natural under the circumstances. If you cut yourself the first thing you do is look for help. It's logical, no?'

Harriet was on a roll. 'Well what about when I asked him if anyone lived in that house or not? He avoided a proper reply.'

John was shaking his head in disbelief. 'No, no, no, not exactly. He implied in a very friendly manner that you shouldn't stick your nose into other people's affairs.' He picked up his book again. 'And I find that perfectly reasonable.'

'That's not the point and you know it.' Harriet was determined to get as much mileage out of this as possible. 'He said he didn't know if the place was inhabited or not, and yet he spends his nights there. Why?'

John was trying to lay the conversation to rest and failing dismally. 'For goodness' sake. Because he probably had a wonderful time with that woman. Or the two women... those two you're so concerned about,' he posited. He was desperately searching for an answer that would staunch Harriet's persistent questioning of a singularly uninteresting situation. 'Or perhaps they live in the house,' he went on. 'Or perhaps he lives there himself. Or somebody does. Oh, how the bloody hell should I know?!'

He saw the look on Harriet's face. She wouldn't be satisfied until they upped sticks and moved on. John got up and put his arms around her from behind. 'Oh, Harriet. Come on...'

There were tears in her eyes. 'No normal person would live in a place like that.'

'No?'

'No.'

John acceded, 'You're probably right, my darling.' He slipped a hand under her sweater. Cupping her right breast, he felt the nipple stiffen to his touch. He nibbled around her earlobe, eliciting a snigger. 'Now, are you coming to bed or am I going to throw you to the floor and rip off all your clothes?'

☼

Miriam and Rupert hadn't returned. Ted guessed that they had retreated to wherever in the house it was that Miriam's bedroom was located. That suited him fine.

Divide and conquer, eh?

Ted smiled wryly to himself. He was sitting up in bed watching Fran disrobe. She removed her gown to reveal matching lacy black brassiere and briefs. Ted felt a tingle in his loins; she really did have the most incredibly sexy body. 'You arouse me more than any woman I've met for a long time,' he said.

Fran eased down her panties and unfastened the brassiere, tossing it to one side. 'Thanks for the compliment,' she said.

The tone suggested she accepted such compliments with a pinch of salt. She probably received them a lot, Ted thought. He said, 'I'm dead serious, Fran. Why else do you think I waited for you today? There were places I should have been, but I simply had to see you again. You intrigue me. And you worry me, because I don't understand you.'

Fran came over to the bed and allowed him to take her in his arms. 'Don't try to,' she said.

As the storm raged outside Farnsworth's dull, grey walls, they made love. It was as passionate and satiating as it had been the first time. Later, as Ted slept, Fran lay silently beside him, staring wide-eyed. But right now sleep eluded her. Ted was snoring; it was barely audible, but snoring nonetheless.

Fran sat up and moved stealthily across the bed. Gone was the beautiful, sophisticated woman, in her place a ravenous, cunning predator. She came to a stop, poised directly above Ted's prone body. Gently, she lowered herself until her full weight was across him. She could feel the flutter of his heartbeat against her breast. Ted stirred slightly and then the snoring sound resumed. Fran waited a full minute before she moved again, reaching over and deftly pulling away the tapes securing the bandage on Ted's arm. As she carefully lifted it up, some blood trickled from the corner of the partially closed-over gash and ran down onto the sheets. Quick as a flash she was on it; with her tongue she followed the trail of the little river back up to its source making sure not to miss any, and then closed her mouth over the ugly wound. She paused, grimacing -

Ugghh! Disinfectant... Oh, well...

- and then started to suck. The flesh on Ted's arm curled back and the plasma began to flow. Fran applied herself to the feed, taking deep swallow after deep swallow, savouring the faintly metallic taste. Ted stirred again, this time raising his head from the pillow. Fran leant up and pressed her mouth to his, smearing it with his own blood. Not really conscious, Ted began to return the kiss but then flopped back down and was immediately asleep again. Fran quickly returned her attention to his arm, supping feverishly upon the welters of red that now flowed freely.

On face value her actions were obscene. Revolting. A perversion of nature. And yet there was a curious eroticism to the act; the fascinatingly arousing manner in which her tongue traced along the line of the cut, the way that her eyes blazed in the rapture of the moment, the fact that her whole body was trembling with ecstasy... At the sound of stumbling footfalls outside the room, Fran froze. She didn't cease her oral ministrations, but noticeably slowed and her breathing became shallow as she listened attentively to the sound. There it was again.

Climbing off the bed and wiping away the juices from her mouth with the back of her hand, she grabbed up a vivid purple robe, slipped it on, and went out into the hallway. At the top of the staircase, slumped across the banisters, Fran recognised Miriam. She stepped towards her: 'Darling, are you alright?'

Miriam lazily turned her head in response to the voice; Fran saw that her face was awash with blood. Her hair was matted with the stuff and it dribbled from her mouth. The eyes were glazed as if she wasn't quite sure who it was speaking to her. Managing to lever herself upright, Miriam swayed on her feet. To all intents and purposes she looked like she'd had a little too much to drink. Ironic, because that was precisely the case. Her gold-spangled gown was torn at the shoulder and ripped along one seam, indicating that the assault had not been so easy this time.

Fran took Miriam's face in her hands and began to

lovingly lick away the blood, dabbing at the corners of Miriam's mouth with the tip of her tongue. 'Darling,' she said, 'where is he?' Miriam just stared at her. Fran gave a her a sharp, stinging slap across the face and repeated the question. The last thing they needed was a replay of the incident several nights ago when that man, Brian, had made a bid for escape. They had been fortunate to find him in the woods, crawling around naked in the pouring rain, deranged, disoriented and on the point of death.

Miriam smiled. 'Don't worry.' She giggled gleefully. 'I took precautions...'

The thing on the bed in Miriam's chamber hardly resembled the man who had driven them home that evening. In fact, it scarcely resembled a man at all. The back was arched, the body twisted, the mouth contorted and gagging in a hideous, soundless scream. The feet were jutting out at unnatural angles; Fran realised that the tarsi had been shattered to prevent him even standing, let alone attempting to negotiate an escape. An admirable precaution, she thought to herself. Every sinew in Rupert's wiry frame strained in conflict with the multiple lacerations that covered his trunk.

Fran swiftly cast off her robe and rushed, naked, to the bed. Miriam was only paces behind, tearing at her own gown and dropping it in rags to the floor. By the time she reached the bed, Fran already had her teeth embedded deeply in the flesh on Rupert's shoulder. A spray of blood speckled her face and she began to drink greedily. Rupert was trying to put up a fight, but the nominal resistance he had left in him after Miriam's initial frenzied assault was dwindling fast. Fran continued to feed, gripping his shoulders and trying to stop him bucking about.

That's it, struggle you bastard. But don't die yet... no fun if you die...

Miriam grabbed a handful of hair and wrenched back Rupert's head, exposing his throat. Snarling like a feral beast, she sank her incisors into the white flesh and a welter of scarlet spewed up over her mouth and dripped from her chin. As she began to drink, she slipped a hand down between her legs and began to stroke herself, slowly at first, then harder and faster. Such was the extent of her stimulation that the result was almost instantaneous; she threw back her head, quivering and squealing with delight as a powerful orgasm coursed through her.

Easing her grip on Rupert, Fran reached for the hunting knife, which was laying at the foot of the bed. The steel blade flashed as it plunged into the man's torso, entering between the second and third rib. His body convulsed and he vomited. Again and again the knife rose and fell, each slash tearing through muscle and sinew and opening up fresh veins whilst skilfully avoiding the main arteries.

Mustn't die yet. No fun if you die...

Miriam was now watching Fran like a devoted puppy dog waiting for its mistress to play fetch-ball, trying to pre-empt just where the blade would fall next and then, with lightning reflexes, extending her tongue and catching the spatters of blood that flew through the air with each slashing motion.

Fran dropped the knife and the two women deliriously grabbed hold of each other, kissing, licking, fondling... The last thing that Rupert saw, before the blackness of death shrouded him forever, was the vision of two very beautiful women with viscera dripping from their fabulous naked bodies, lost in the throes of a passionate embrace, passing a mouthful of blood - *his* blood - back and forth between each other, as young lovers might playfully do with a sampling of wine.

Seizing the knife again, Fran was about to continue the assault, but Miriam reached out and stopped her. She said, quietly, 'No more, Fran. No more. He's dead.' Heedless, Fran began to stab at the corpse, the knife grinding against bone with each now less measured thrust. Miriam made a grab for Fran's wrist and, with her other hand, gently prised the white-knuckled fingers from around the hasp. Taking the knife from her, Miriam's eyes glittered in the darkness. 'Let's finish up with a real treat,' she said. With a squeal, she dug the knife deeply into Rupert's crotch, twisting the blade as she did so. It tore open his scrotum, severed one of the sperm tubes and found its mark in the external iliac artery. A fountain of dark fluid erupted from the rended conduit and began pooling on the bedclothes. His dead body jerked in a reflex action as the two women got down between his legs and started to drink.

Gradually the blood-lust subsided and, pushing the limp, ragged piece of meat that had once been a man named Rupert onto the floor, the two women collapsed on the bed in a sated embrace. Holding each other tightly, they mutually soothed and calmed until their breathing was under control.

'Hell, that was good,' Miriam sighed.

Twenty minutes later, had Ted been awake, he would probably have heard a bumping sound in the hallway. Had he investigated, he would have been horrified to see two naked women, drenched in blood, hulking a hideously mutilated cadaver - the flesh hanging in tatters from its bones - down the stairwell. As it was, he slept on, blissfully unaware of the heinous murder that had been committed by the two mysterious, beguiling women... one of whom he was falling in love with.

IX

CRASH

Less than an hour later, Miriam was standing in the wide, old-fashioned bathtub, watching the swirls of red disappearing down the plug hole and luxuriating in the purifying properties of the scalding water.

The removal of Rupert's body had been messy - though in truth no messier than these necessities always were - and they had deposited the him and his car near the usual spot, cutting through the woods and getting back to the house a little after 1.30.

Fran stepped into the tub beside Miriam, angled the shower head towards herself and turned up her face to greet the pinpoints of spray. Eyes closed, she smiled at the feel of Miriam's soft, soapy hands massaging away the caked-on gore. They took it in turns to lick at each other's faces, as animals do during the act of grooming one another, dabbing away all the little traces of dried blood. The combination of the hot water and succour worked to chaperone away the obscene mess until both Fran and Miriam's bodies had been cleansed of all traces of the crime. Fran sighed and leant back against the white tiling. Tonight's kill had been the most exhilarating and satisfying yet. 'Make love to me, darling' she whispered.

Miriam knelt down in the tub and dotted Fran's glistening abdomen with delicate kisses, whilst her hands crept around and grasped hold of her bottom. Then she dipped her head and forced her face in between Fran's thighs.

Oh my God, that's heaven...

Fran sobbed with pleasure as she felt the tongue go to work in her most private place.

'You're playing a dangerous game, Fran.' Miriam's voice drifted up through the sea of pleasure. 'Kill him before it's too late. Kill him!'

Fran felt the hands part her buttocks and she shuddered as a soapy finger circled the tight ring of her anus. 'Please... don't stop!' she gasped. Miriam's middle finger cautiously navigated its way through the resistance of the sphincter and slipped into the warm recesses of Fran's bowels. The burning sensation as breathtaking pleasure merged with exquisite pain made her cry out. Miriam began to move her finger in and out of the tight orifice as if it were a small penis, whilst her strong tongue continued to knead the fragrant flesh between Fran's legs, eagerly swallowing down the abundance of nectar that leaked from the vermilion slit.

Later they lay at opposite ends of the tub, immersed in steaming, pine-scented water. 'I meant it, Fran,' Miriam said. 'You have to kill him.' Fran dreamily cupped her hands and filled them with bubbles, watching the soapy water seep out between her fingers. 'Are you listening to me?' Miriam said angrily. 'It's my house and I won't let him stay here.' She saw the expression on Fran's face change and immediately regretted her choice of words. Her tone softened. 'I didn't mean that. It's *our* house. But look, darling, can't you see how dangerous this is? You're fooling with fire. There's only one way to play this game, I know it and you know it. We feed, we kill, we dispose of. It's a recipe for danger the way it is, but anything else could be disastrous. You *must* kill him.'

'I will,' Fran said. 'But not yet.'

Miriam's eyes watered up. 'Why?' She already knew the answer.

'Because right now I need him. Men don't mean a thing to you. You wouldn't care a damn if you never slept with a man again. But I'm not like you and I've never pretended to be. Occasionally I need male company.'

A tear trickled down Miriam's face. She roughly brushed it away. 'Is it better?'

Fran smiled. 'No, my darling, it's not better. And it's not worse. It's just different.' That didn't seem to provide Miriam with a great deal of consolation; the tears welled up and began to flow. Fran leaned forward and gently kissed them away. 'The things we do...' she began. 'What we are... the way we've been forced to exist - yes, I say exist, because it's an existence, not a life. We didn't choose it to be this way. The choice was made for us. And it's a malediction of ungodly proportions. But we have each other and we always will. You're the only thing that makes this whole worthless existence bearable, Miriam. You're my anchor. My sanity. I will always, and I mean *always*, love you. You've stolen my heart and you know it. You mean more to me than any lousey man ever could. Good God, I left a man I'd been with for over two years just to be with you, didn't I?' She laughed at the irony. 'And look what resulted from that!

'But all that said, there's something about this man and I need him around right now. And there's no reason to be concerned, he won't cause us any problems. He's well and truly hooked. I assure you, when the time is right he *will* be killed. I shall kill him. But not now. Not yet. Can you understand that?'

Miriam was pouting like the little girl refused a lollipop by a stern parent. 'No, I can't understand it,' she said. Her mouth curved into a forgiving half-smile. 'But I accept it. For now at least. I know who he is and I can guess why you're keeping him alive. Just remember though, there is a saying that before setting out on revenge you should first dig two graves.'

Fran smiled. 'Most erudite, my darling. I shall certainly bear that in mind. But let's not forget something here. I'm already dead.'

✻

It was some time just before dawn when Harriet awoke. Having been disturbed in the early hours by the sound of a car, she had been unable to get back to sleep for some time and what little she did get was subsequently fitful. Now she was longing to get away from the increasing tension and claustrophobia of the caravan and fill her lungs with fresh air. She quietly got dressed, pulled her favourite waist-length brown cardigan from the closet, popped on the green woolly hat that her mother had knitted for her last Christmas, and slipped out into the bracing air. The sun was only just up and it shone blindingly through the trees. Harriet inhaled deeply and caught her breath; it was somewhat colder than she'd anticipated. She wondered if she should go back inside and fetch her fleece-lined overcoat and maybe a scarf. On the one hand she knew she'd warm up once she started walking, but then again it really was most bitterly cold. As she paused, weighing up the situation, out of the corner of her eye she caught a movement near the trees over in the direction of the big house. She turned her head and looked but couldn't see anything.

Probably just a bird... or an animal... or...

Then she saw them. Harriet felt her stomach tighten as she spotted the two women hurrying through the woods, and all thoughts of returning to the caravan vanished.

Right. Let's see just where it is you're going...

She set off in the direction of the trees.

...but just make sure that they don't see you.

Endeavouring to maintain a safe distance of at least fifty yards between herself and her quarry, Harriet dodged in an out of the gnarled trees and low-hanging branches, her breathing becoming more laboured by the moment; wherever it was these women were headed, they weren't wasting any time and Harriet was having difficulty keeping up with them. Her circumspection, prudent as it might have been, was apparently unwarranted, for not once did either of the women give any indication of an awareness that they were being watched. They hurried swiftly along, weaving their way through the trees with a practiced familiarity of the territory. From time to time Harriet cursed under her breath as she lost sight of them for a few moments, but then there they would be again. She slipped on wet leaves and stumbled over mossy hillocks, and at one point was lucky not to twist her ankle when she stepped into a small pothole that was obscured from sight by the carpet of dead foliage.

In spite of her intense curiosity, Harriet had to admit to herself that she felt a bit ridiculous playing spy. The further she went into the woods, the less certain she became that this had been such a smart idea. A couple of times she thought about turning back, but the monotonous chiming of the church bell somewhere off ahead had an agreeably calming effect on her trepidation and she pressed on. The bottom line was that if she didn't find out once and for all what these women were up to, she was convinced she would be driven stark staring mad!

Crossing a narrow ghyll, she again lost sight of them. Harriet stopped and listened. Over the pounding of the blood in her ears, all she could hear was the woodland chorus. She looked around her, but the women were nowhere to be seen.

Shit!

The best she could do now was to keep going in the direction she'd last seen them and hope for the best. Moving even more cautiously now and feeling the tendrils of fear begin to worm inside her, she quickened her pace.

Then, quite unexpectedly, the woods ended and she found herself standing at the edge of a graveyard. An ocean of dilapidated stone fanned out before her. Harriet had always hated cemeteries; they were frightening places. Having had to stand and watch her father being buried when she was just ten years old probably hadn't helped a great deal. Sure, she could understand how someone would wish to mark the passing of a loved one in some way. But she found the notion of indifferent passers-by, idly whiling away an hour or two reading the chiselled lamentations earnestly bestowed by the broken-hearted upon a beloved Gladys or a greatly missed William, thoroughly ghoulish. Some of the crumbling monuments to the dead standing here looked as if they might be centuries old. Those that had buried them had probably long since been buried themselves, Harriet thought.

She gingerly picked her way through the maze of headstones. In the distance, through the trees, she could see the church, but of the two women there wasn't a trace. The sound of the bell ceased abruptly and the churchyard was shrouded in silence. Even the sound of birdsong was suddenly conspicuous by its absence.

☼

At the same time that Harriet was making her way back through the woods from the cemetery, Ted Gorman was running for a train. He took the steps leading down to the platform two at a time and, as he hastened along the length of the train, he caught sight of his mother waving at him from a doorway in the end carriage. He made it to the step and smiled up at her but, as she reached out a hand to help him aboard, the train started to move. He grabbed hold of the handrail on the open door but they were already gathering speed at an alarming rate. He tried desperately to get a footing but he couldn't. He knew he should let go before it was too late, but his mother was saying something to him and he couldn't make out the words. Suddenly the train hurtled into the blackness of night. The icy wind tore at him and the door swung back and forth wildly; it took every ounce of his strength for Ted to hang on. The muscles in his arms were screaming at him and he could feel his grip beginning to slacken. He looked up at his mother who, for some banal reason, wasn't his mother any longer. She was Fran and she was laughing. Couldn't she see what was happening here? Letting go of the rail with one hand, he tried to stretch out to her but couldn't quite reach. In that single moment he knew that he was going to die. He could feel himself slipping and he began to cry. Now Fran was his mother again and she was crying too. 'I love you, mum.' he managed to say. 'I love you...'

At the instant Ted lost hold of the rail, his eyes snapped open.

There was a sickening, twisting sensation in his gut and he realised that his cheeks were wet. He lay still on the bed, picturing the last moments of the dream and staving off an overwhelming compulsion to burst into tears.

Now what the hell was all that about?

His mother was dead - she had passed away within weeks of his father. But just when was the last time he had taken the time to visit the grave?

That's something to be rectified at the earliest opportunity, old boy.

Noting with some annoyance that he was once again alone in the bed, Ted sat up, massaging his aching limbs. He felt even worse than he had done the day before. Excessive sleep can have the same enfeebling results as sleep deprivation, worse perhaps. The muscles slacken from lack of exercise and the ligaments tighten as the body slips into a state of neglect.

Ted's arm was hurting more than ever. Added to that, the bandage had come loose in the night and the wound had evidently been bleeding again.

Shaking off the morbid conjurings of his dream, he was suddenly aware of an uncomfortable sensation working its way up from the pit of his stomach. He recognised the feeling immediately. Often when he was busy he would skip lunch, with the inevitability that by mid-afternoon this feeling would descend on him and he would end up having to stop to eat anyway. Biology had never been Ted's strong suit but, as he understood it, the human stomach contained a hideous sounding cocktail of hydrochloric acid, rennin, pepsin, and other chemicals that serve to break down food in the process of digestion. In the absence of anything substantial to work on, his gastric juices were inclined to tackle the lining of the stomach, with the short-term result being severe discomfort and nausea. Long term? Probably a peptic ulcer.

When had he last eaten anyway? Yesterday? Two days ago? Ted realised he couldn't even remember. 'Christ, I'm hungry,' he said aloud. 'I could murder a fish supper.'

He reached out and picked up his watch. Not working. Of course. The taste in his mouth was vile. He peered hopefully into the goblets on the table. His was empty but there was a drop left in Fran's. He swilled it around his mouth and sucked it in and out through his teeth a couple of times.

Now that's one superior mouthwash.

Dragging himself up off the bed, Ted went to the window. As he looked out he caught sight of the dim reflection of his face in the glass. Great grief, did he look as awful as he thought he did? He felt his chin. He hadn't shaved for days either. He cast a look around the room. That was odd. He hadn't really paid much attention before, but now that he thought about it he realised that it was devoid of a mirror.

A lady's boudoir without a vanity mirror? Unheard of!

On the wall in the corner, beside the door, he noticed something covered with a sheet of black cloth. As he got closer he realised that it wasn't actually cloth, it was paper and the top edge was frayed. Taking hold of it he tore downward and a long strip ripped off in his hand revealing the dirty surface of a mirror.

Why on earth...?

✳

By the time Harriet got back to the caravan, John was up, dressed and frying eggs. The transistor radio was blaring; it was the recently re-released Gary Puckett classic "Young Girl". John was singing along to it. Badly. Since he didn't ask, Harriet decided it was probably best not to mention what she'd been up to. John was being obstinate enough about all this as it was and there was nothing to be achieved by fanning the flames.

Gary Puckett finished and Frankie Vaughn came on. Harriet scowled and switched it off.

As they sat down in the window to eat, away in the distance they both heard the sound of a motor turning over. A minute later Ted's car passed nearby. Harriet saw him look and waved. Ted raised a hand in acknowledgement. Harriet opened her mouth to speak, but John cut her off. He wagged a finger in the air: 'I don't know and I don't care,' he said with a grin.

Once he'd cleared the mud track and got out into the lane, Ted pressed down hard on the accelerator and the BMW roared off. He knew that inevitably he would return to see Fran again, but for now his sole intention was to head for The Wayfarer, get something hot to eat and see if he could bribe someone - that pretty little desk clerk, perhaps - to let him use one of the guest bathrooms. He'd toyed briefly with the idea of descending on that nice Bailey couple in the caravan, but concluded that it might have been one intrusion too many, especially as they'd already gone beyond the call of duty in coping with his emergency yesterday.

Ted had only travelled about a mile, and had just taken a sharp bend rather recklessly, when he was forced to slam on the brakes to avoid hitting a police car parked diagonally across the road in front of him. A little way ahead it looked as if there had been some sort of accident. Ted couldn't really see what had happened, but the presence of two police cars and an ambulance implied that it wasn't anything trivial.

He stopped the car and got out. As he made his way round the side of the police car he saw what the problem was. A metallic red Rover had ploughed into the ditch and it looked to Ted pretty much like a write-off. One of the policemen was in the process of prising open the driver's side door. As he did so, a naked, blood-streaked leg flopped out. Ted saw that it was all but severed from the torso, attached only by a single, sinewy thread. He glimpsed partially denuded bone, the flesh hanging from it in tattered strips. Grimacing, Ted turned up his collar against the cold.

Nasty. Very nasty.

Feeling for his carton of Rothmans, he pressed one between his lips and was just about to light it as the two ambulance men were carefully lifting the body from the car onto a stretcher. Ted stared in horror. His mouth fell open and the unlit cigarette dropped to the ground. The corpse being lifted out of the car was Rupert. Or at least what was left of Rupert. His bedraggled body looked as if it had been run through a mangle.

Ted felt faint. He put a hand against the police car to

steady himself. At that moment one of the officers spotted him and came hurrying over. 'Please, sir, there's nothing for you to see here. Go back to your car, the road will be clear in a few minutes.' He stopped as he saw the ghastly pallor on Ted's face. 'I say, are you alright sir?' Ted managed to mumble something in the affirmative and slowly made his way back to the BMW. He climbed in and slammed the door, his mind racing. Thoughts of food and personal hygiene were now buried beneath a solitary pressing aim. He had to get back to the house and let Miriam and Fran know what had happened to poor Rupert.

It took him less that five minutes to reach Farnsworth Hall. Standing in the dark hallway, he tried to gather his thoughts, but he felt dizzy. There'd be no point looking around upstairs, there wouldn't be anybody around, that was for sure.

Okay then, let's try downstairs.

At the end of the hall there was a large panelled door. It looked far too big to lead to a closet space. Ted tried the handle, half expecting it to be locked, but to his surprise it opened. A flight of stairs led down into the darkness. He struck a match and made his way carefully downwards. The steps turned back on themselves and ended at another door. It looked like it was made of solid oak and there was no way that Ted would have got through it had it been locked. But it too opened freely. Suddenly he felt the spent match burning the tip of his fingers and he cursed, angrily blowing it out and dropping it to the floor. Striking another, he stepped through door.

Inside, Ted found himself standing at one end of a long, draughty, white brick tunnel. Moisture dripped from the walls. This could only lead to the cellar, he thought. Hesitating for a moment, he began to make his way along it, shielding the naked flame from the draught with a cupped hand and watching the eerie, flickering patterns on the white brickwork. Then, from out of nowhere, a blast of cold air rushed through the tunnel. Ted heard the door slam shut behind him and the match went out. He struck another and retraced his steps. As he reached for the wrought iron latch and lifted it, unbelievably it snapped off. He stared down incredulously at the broken piece of metal in his hand.

Fuck!

Left with little choice but to investigate the other end of the tunnel, Ted struck a fourth match and set off. As he had suspected, it led down to the fabled cellar. And, just as Miriam had bragged, it was absolutely heaving with rack upon rack of dusty bottles of the finest wine. Ted stood in awe. The house might be a wreck but these ladies certainly knew how to live well.

Just before the match died, he spotted a table and chairs in the corner. And candles too! He stood in the pitch blackness and shook the packet of matches. There were only a couple left. Best not to waste any. With his hands stretched out and waving back and forth in front of him, he made his way carefully through the darkness in the direction of the table. There he felt for one of the candles, struck another match and soon the corner of the cellar was bathed in a sickly yellow glow.

Slumping down on one of the chairs, he lit a cigarette in the dancing flame of the candle and, with a tired sigh, exhaled a plume of smoke. Nothing to do now but wait. And just hope that Fran - wherever the hell she was - came back soon.

X

FIRST CONTACT

As the sun began to dip in the sky over Farnsworth, aside from the chattering of the birds, the only sound discernible to Harriet's ears was the soft brushing of paint on canvas. She was standing at the edge of the trees about a hundred yards from the house. In front of her was an easel upon which rested a 6 ft. by 3 ft. canvas. Upon the canvas was a very respectable portrait of Farnsworth Hall. It was coming along in leaps and bounds and although she'd modestly laughed off John's compliments at lunchtime, secretly Harriet was rather pleased with her efforts.

She paused in her toil and stared fixedly at the grey walls of the edifice. It was a truly magnificent piece of architecture and yet there was something indefinably malevolent about it. Harriet, her imagination working overtime, saw it as a living entity, a deadly colossus with savage tendrils that, should she deign to get too close, would snake out, enfold her and tear her mind apart.

Now what a painting that would make...

Harriet smiled to herself. She decided that a trip into the village to enquire about a local library might prove valuable, then she could see what could be found out about the place. Provided, that is, John could be inveigled away from his precious fishing rod for five minutes. It was too late to contemplate today, but maybe first thing tomorrow morning.

The snap of a twig brought Harriet out of her thoughts. She looked around and surveyed the trees behind her. There was nothing untoward to be seen. Deciding it was probably some small woodland animal or another, she returned her attention to the painting. The light was going fast now. A few more minutes and she'd have to think about packing up for the day, or John would be coming to look for her.

A little more olive was needed in the shadowed areas of the ivy that clad the right-hand wall. She picked out the smallest brush from her extensive selection and, moving in very close, began to carefully apply little splotches of colour to the canvas. She was concentrating so hard that she didn't even notice that the birdsong had ceased. A rustling sound behind her broke through her concentration. Turning her head, she half expected to see John standing, hands on hips, playfully demanding to know why his dinner wasn't ready.

Harriet stood bolt upright. Stepping out of the trees, not ten feet away, Fran and Miriam walked straight over and stopped in front of her. How the hell she hadn't heard them coming Harriet didn't know. But now she could feel herself beginning to tremble and prayed that the terror gripping her wasn't externally apparent. She needn't have been too concerned, for both women were staring at the painting of the house. If only the expressions on their faces reflected admiration of Harriet's artistic talents; instead there was puzzlement, as if neither of them were sure why anyone would be standing here painting a picture of their house. If it even was their house.

Harriet tried to control her fear. It wasn't as if she were in danger. Surely the worst thing they could do was deliver a stiff warning to get off their land. And that would suit Harriet just fine.

Fran turned and, reaching up, she pressed her thumb to Harriet's forehead. 'I always knew we'd find each other,' she said, moving her thumb up, then down and across. 'By this sign I'll recognise you.' All at once Harriet felt her trembling subside and she became calm. Calmer, in fact, than she had been in days. More than that, she felt an inner peace, a tranquillity unlike anything she could recall ever experiencing before in her life. Fran gave her a final look filled with fierce hatred and then, as silently as they had arrived, the two women turned and walked away towards the house.

Harriet stared after them and, as they disappeared around the side of the house, the fear came gushing back and she began to shake more violently than before. As quickly as she could, she gathered up her things and hurried back to the caravan. John hadn't returned yet and it was cold inside. She thought about going to find him but changed her mind; any remarks he might have to make upon hearing her account of what had just happened weren't likely to be favourable. Instead she switched on both bars on the compact electric heater and went into the bathroom. Standing in front of the mirror, she inspected her brow. There wasn't any sign of a blemish or indentation where Fran had touched her, but there was a very palpable tingling sensation. The words came back to her... 'By this sign I'll recognise you'... What the hell did that mean? Harriet shivered.

Stripping off her clothes, she stepped into the little shower cubicle and turned the water on full. Then she picked up a bar of Imperial Leather soap and began to scrub vigorously at her forehead.

☼

From his prison deep in the recesses of Farnsworth Hall, Ted had born witness to numerous noises from upstairs throughout the course of the day. Each time he had pounded on the door and hollered for help, and each time no-one had come. Now, once again, he was sure he had heard the slam of a door and the sound of footfalls. 'Hey,' he yelled, hammering his closed fist hard against the oak door. 'Is anybody there? Open up!' He paused and listened, expecting silence, but instead the sound of footsteps came closer. There was someone on the staircase outside. 'Fran? Is that you Fran? Open the door!' The footsteps stopped and to Ted's relief the handle rattled and the door swung open. Fran was standing looking inquiringly at him. Miriam was a few feet behind her on the steps.

'What on earth happened?' Fran asked with a trace of amusement that immediately raised Ted's hackles.

He said, a little more tersely than he intended, 'What the bloody hell does it look like?' He had never been much of a stoic. 'The wind blew the door shut and the handle broke off.'

'What on earth made you come down here?'

Yes, that was definitely amusement in her tone. But Ted had to admit to himself that it wasn't an unreasonable question. He suddenly felt a little bit stupid.

'Well, I... I was looking for you,' he said sheepishly.

'Are you alright?'

Ted adopted the look of an injured, sympathy-seeking child. 'I've been locked down here all day,' he mumbled. 'It's cold and damp. And I was getting worried that you weren't coming back.'

Fran smiled warmly. 'Come on. Let's get you something to drink.'

'Oh, and there's something else,' Ted said, mild suspicion creeping into his voice. 'Do you know that your friend - that Rupert fellow who was here last night - is dead?'

Miriam, who had remained silent until now, stared at him. 'Dead?'

Ted couldn't be certain if there was surprise there or not. And if there was, was it surprise at the terrible news or surprise that he even knew about it? He continued, 'Yes, dead. I saw his car on the road this morning. Bad accident.'

Miriam was attempting to look regretful. 'He didn't look too fit as he left last night,' she said. 'I told him to drive carefully. He'd had too much to drink.'

'That's terrible,' Fran chipped in. 'Poor Rupert.'

Surprised or otherwise, there certainly didn't seem to be a great deal of concern here, Ted thought. But then again, if Rupert had been merely another ship passing in the night, why should there be? Fran had introduced Rupert to him as Miriam's "friend" - which Ted had taken to mean casual pick-up, as indeed he himself had been - and so why should they get emotional over his demise? Anyway, all Ted wanted right now was to get out of the damned cellar. He said so.

'Come on,' Fran smiled. 'I'll take you upstairs.'

'Good,' said Ted. 'And then there are a few things I'd like you to explain to me.'

Twenty minutes later, feeling not particularly fortified by the two glasses of red wine that he had emptied into himself, Ted flopped down on the bed. Fran kissed him and helped him out of his clothes, then removed her own. A feeling of immense tiredness descended upon him and, as Fran crossed over to the bed, he felt his eyelids beginning to sag. There were so many questions that needed answering, but for the moment -

Got to rest my eyes... questions later... got to sleep...

- 'I'm sorry,' he started to say, 'I don't think I'm going to be much good to you right now. I need to...' His words trailed off as sleep engulfed him.

Sex was the last thing on Fran's mind as primordial instinct took over and she climbed naked atop his prone body. Bending her head to his arm, she bit deeply into the wound and greedily began to consume the dark fluid that oozed out. Abandoning herself completely to the feed, Fran became so absorbed that she failed to hear the bedroom door opening. Miriam, wearing a black lace negligee, stood in the doorway watching Fran, the emotions of bitter jealousy and raging hunger waging a war in her head.

Suddenly aware of another presence in the room, Fran looked up. Her mouth was daubed with blood, her face etched with guilt. Miriam frowned; just like the little girl caught stealing ice cream, she thought. The two women stared at each other for a moment and then, without a word, Fran reached down, lifted Ted's arm and held it out towards Miriam.

A peace offering?

Miriam's expression of parental disapproval melted into a fond smile. She walked to the bed and knelt down. As Fran applied pressure on either side of the grotesque slash on Ted's arm, Miriam bowed her head and tasted some of the blood that surged forth. It was good. Very good in fact. She looked up at Fran who leaned over and kissed her hard. Ted meanwhile remained oblivious to it all, so deeply lost in his world of sleep as to be practically comatose.

For the next five minutes Miriam's attention vacillated

between the sweet sustenance running from Ted's arm and the tender ministrations of Fran's lips against hers. Then she stood up and stepped away from the bed. Removing her negligee, underneath which she was naked, her firm, impertinent breasts jutted invitingly towards Fran. Miriam ran her hands across her waist and over her hips, delighting in the sensuous feel of her own silky skin.

She padded back over to the bed, sat down on the edge and took Fran in her arms. 'Only a woman knows what another woman really needs, darling,' she said. Her eyes twinkled. 'I'll show you what true love is all about.'

Usually submissive to her little blonde angel's caresses, now it was Fran who took the initiative. 'No, my sweet Miriam,' she said. 'Let me show *you*.' Beginning at the ankle, she planted a flurry of tender fairy kisses up Miriam's left leg, working across the milky white of her thigh and leaving a little trail of red from the blood on her mouth.

For more than an hour they made fulfilling, rhapsodic love as they never had before, doing everything that it is possible for two women to do for one another. Afterwards, as they lay in each other's arms, Miriam delicately kissed Fran's closed eyelids.

Fran smiled. 'That was wonderful.'

'It's about to get better, my darling' Miriam giggled mischievously. 'I'll show you that you don't need any man around.' Rolling over, she reached down into the cabinet beside the bed and withdrew a black harness with a pink rubber attachment resembling a male appendage.

Fran's eyes widened with excitement as Miriam began to strap herself into the harness. 'Oh, God, yes...'

Though neither of them was aware of it, Ted had partially regained consciousness. He lay face up on the edge of the bed, bleary-eyed and unsure of where he was. He turned his head to one side. Later he would conclude that what he'd seen must surely have been the product of some wild, delirium-induced fantasy. But right now it seemed real enough. What he saw, though unfocussed and hazy, was Miriam climbing between Fran's splayed legs. Nothing too abnormal about that per se. Except that Miriam appeared to have a penis which Fran was begging her to insert...

The room began to spin and the light grew very, very bright, and Ted returned to the safe womb of unconsciousness.

XI

THE HOUSE ON HAUNTED HILL

Miriam opened her eyes, blinking away the dreams. What time was it? It was still dark, or at least appeared to be; the thick velvet curtains were drawn so it was hard to tell. But it still felt like night.

After they had made love for the second time, she and Fran had snuggled down under the blankets like spoons, front to back, and both of them had drifted into a deep sleep. Which was where Fran still seemed to be residing now. Ted lay on the far side of the bed. He too was asleep. Miriam nuzzled in closer to Fran and lightly kissed the back of her neck. The regular breathing faltered for a moment and then resumed.

Damn!

Miriam was suddenly filled with the need to go to the bathroom. She tried to think about something else but that was a pointless exercise. Sighing, she climbed from beneath the covers, picked out one of Fran's gowns - a particularly attractive one patterned in gold lace - and slipped it on. It was a little too large for her, but served its immediate purpose. Quietly opening the bedroom door, she made her way down the corridor to the bathroom, but as she passed the sitting room she caught sight of a glimmer of light from beneath the door. She reached out and pushed it open. Panic gripped her as blinding light flooded out into the hall. Natural light. Sunlight!

Christ, it's day...

She rushed across the room to the curtains and pulled them together, shutting out the glare. Then she ran back to the bedroom and, grabbing Fran by the shoulders, shook her aggressively. Fran continued to stare, unblinking, lost in that dreamy waking sleep.

'Fran! Fran, it's day. Wake up, for God's sake, it's day!'

There was no reaction. Miriam managed to get her arms underneath Fran's armpits and, linking her hands together at the front, with an almighty effort she levered her up off the bed. 'Darling, we have to move right now. Can you hear me? It's day!' At last the urgency in Miriam's pleas penetrated the wall behind which Fran's consciousness had retired. Murmuring incoherently, she just about took her own weight on her feet and, with Miriam's help, shakily managed to get her arms into her gown. By the time she was dressed she was more or less *compos mentis* again.

They rushed through the house to the back door, but as Fran reached for the handle, Miriam screamed at her, 'No! It's too late. Too bright...' Without hesitation they turned and ran down the hall to the basement door. With Miriam close on her heels, Fran took the steps at speed and together they disappeared down the tunnel to the wine cellar.

✻

Harriet had woken early, as indeed she had done every morning of the duration of their stay at Farnsworth. Haunted all night by her encounter the previous afternoon, today, she had decided, was going to be the day that she appeased her curiosity once and for all. Much to her chagrin, John had pooh-poohed her suggestion of a little investigative trip into the village, so there was only one option open to her that she could see and that was to go to the house and, if necessary, speak with whoever she found there. She had absolutely no idea what she was going to say, but all being well the words would come when the moment arrived.

It had taken a few minutes whilst she got dressed to pluck up the courage and now, having left John sleeping, she neared the house with some considerable trepidation. Not entirely sure that she was doing the right thing, she was nevertheless convinced that, for the sake of her sanity, it was the only thing left to do. Forefront in her mind, although she was trying not to dwell on it too much, was the fact that for the first time since they'd come here she hadn't seen the two women in the grounds that morning. And she knew for sure that they'd gone into the house the night before. Which either meant that she had missed their departure or they were still inside. That unnerved her even more. Fortunately she had seen that man Ted's car parked outside and she was hoping that if the moment of confrontation came it would be him she had to deal with. He'd seemed pleasant enough after all.

Harriet circled the house completely before eventually harnessing the nerve to approach one of the front windows. She pulled away some of the leafy ivy that clung to the frame. The glass was caked in grime. Pulling out a handkerchief, she bunched it up and moistened it with spittle, then dabbed away enough of the dirt to allow her to see inside. Cautiously she pressed her face to the glass but all that there was to see was an empty room with rather filthy walls. She walked over to the door and, taking a deep breath, tried the handle. It was locked. Feeling both disappointment and relief at the same time, she cast a glance over in the direction of the caravan. There was no sign of movement. John was probably still asleep. Wouldn't he be proud of her, plucking up the courage to face her fears?

No, he wouldn't actually. He'd be bloody furious.

Making her way round to the back of the house, she approached the door. Reaching for the handle, to her combined terror and elation, it opened. Breathing hard, she went inside and found herself standing in the dingy hallway.

Christ, this place looks like something out of a Vincent Price movie.

In spite of the tension, Harriet permitted herself a small smile at the analogy. More "The House on Haunted Hill" than that awful thing John had dragged her to see last month - what was it called again? - "Percy's Progress"?

Ugh!

At the foot of the stairs she stopped and looked down the hall, then up the staircase, then back down the hall, trying to determine which was the lesser of the two evils. Deciding that she didn't feel quite brave enough to be caught prowling around upstairs in someone else's house -

Like it doesn't matter so much if I'm caught prowling around downstairs!

- she elected to explore the rooms nearby instead. Walking over to a door on her left, she tapped on it and called out. 'Hello?' Her voice echoed down the hall but there was no reply. She tried again. Silence. The door was locked, so she moved over to the other side and the door that led to the cellar.

Feeling a little bit sick, as quietly as she could Harriet made her way down the steps to another door. This one was wide open. She peered inside and was about to call out again when she thought better of it. Walking through the door, she found herself at the end of a long, white brick tunnel. She could hear water dripping somewhere off in the darkness, and the walls were damp to the touch.

Harriet hesitated, waiting for her eyes to adjust to the gloom. There was a squalling tension building in the pit of her stomach and a tingling in her bladder. The last time she had experienced the sensation she had been a little girl. And suddenly she was twelve years old again, crouched low in the bushes, playing hide-and-seek in the dark. The adrenaline-fuelled fusion of excitement and fear swept through her and she had the overwhelming urge to urinate. Barely able to continue, yet incapable of turning back, Harriet felt her chest tighten and her breathing turned to short gasps. Her mouth and lips felt dry; she tried to lubricate them but her salivary glands had closed up shop.

The cold draught in the tunnel whispered through the follicles on her head and Harriet would have sworn she could actually feel the bristles on the back of her neck rising. She nervously took a couple of paces forward, drawn onwards by... by what? She didn't know, but whatever it was she was now quite certain that the answer to this whole crazy enigma was waiting for her down here. Nevertheless, it took her the best part of three minutes to cover the short distance leading to the cellar; every few steps she stopped and listened, expecting at any moment to be caught in the glare of a flashlight from behind which an angry voice would demand to know just what the hell she thought she was doing.

What she saw when she eventually stepped out from between two tall, wooden racks laden with bottles certainly wasn't what she had imagined. Weak illumination was provided by a candle on a table beside the back wall, though much of the room was masked behind inky shadows. A moth flittered playfully around the candle, seeking comfort in the heat and light, dipping so close to the naked flame that at any moment its gossamer wings might explode in a little puff of fire. Beside the table, partially hidden by another rack was a sofa bed, upon which the tall, chestnut-haired woman was reclined beneath a black mantle. Asleep? For one brief moment Harriet thought she might be dead. But as she moved closer she caught evidence of life in the shallow intakes and exhalations.

'The sleep of the dead,' Harriet whispered under her breath, feeling the gooseflesh rise up along her arms. She stood inspecting the woman for a moment, hardly daring to breathe herself for fear of disturbing the vision of beauty. Oh yes, she was very beautiful, there as no denying that. In fact she wouldn't have looked the least bit out of place on a television commercial for hairspray or make-up.

Though every ounce of sense in her being told Harriet not to do it, she couldn't resist reaching out and lifting up the edge of the mantle. She took a sharp breath in, for beneath the cloth the woman was naked.

My God, she's lovely.

As she stood admiring Fran's body, Harriet's Sapphic dream and the emotions that it had stirred in her came flooding back, and she felt a biting desire to bend down and run her hands over the inviting, forbidden flesh.

Who are you? Why am I so fascinated by you? Oh, my God, I want to touch you so badly...

Common sense prevailed and Harriet carefully lowered the mantle back over the sleeping woman. At the same moment she realised with some surprise that she didn't feel frightened any more. Apprehensive, certainly, but not frightened. There was nothing to fear here, was there? *Was* there?

Had Harriet noticed the figure huddled low in the shadow of the apse on the opposite wall - its eyes now watching her intently from beneath the hood of its cape - she might not have been so assured.

Whilst Fran had fallen asleep immediately upon reaching the sanctuary of the basement, Miriam had remained awake, curled up protectively alongside her lover's legs like the devoted animal that she was. Her head spinning with the dangers of keeping this Ted man around, she had heard the footfalls in the tunnel and hastily scurried over into the apse like a frightened mouse. She had anticipated the prowler to be Ted, but instead the woman that Fran had spoken to in the grounds yesterday had stepped out from the passage. Now, not quite sure how great a threat this woman posed, without Fran's guidance Miriam decided that furtive was best. She moved quietly out of the alcove and edged cautiously along the wall, eyes fixed firmly on Harriet, who had her back to Miriam and appeared to be totally preoccupied with Fran. When she reached the end of the wall, Miriam slipped beneath a brick arch and into the main storage space of the cellar.

Harriet meanwhile was so wrapped up in the curiosity she was expending on Fran that it hadn't even occurred to her that the other woman wasn't here. When the thought did strike, it did so with such suddenness that the burst of terror it deposited in her stomach almost made Harriet retch. She stepped away from Fran and, nervously looking around her, backed across the room and ducked through the arch. She knew little to nothing about wine, but the sheer number of racks filled with bottles here was something to be admired. In spite of her agitation, she couldn't help but muse over where on earth it had all come from and just who exactly was going to drink it.

There must be over five hundred bottles or more down here.

Although she wasn't consciously aware of the piercing blue eyes that were studying her through the gap between two racks near the far wall, the feeling of ill ease in Harriet's subconscious was increasing by the second. All at once she

95

knew she had to get out. Immediately! Following her instincts, without looking back, she ran through the archway and took flight down the tunnel to the door. The wind, wherever the hell it was coming from, was blowing directly into Harriet's face and her eyes were watering. Suddenly she lost her footing on the wet flagstones and plunged headfirst to the ground. Struggling to her feet, she fumbled with the handle on the door - she knew for sure she hadn't closed it behind her when she came in - and that was when she heard the noise in the tunnel behind her. Barely restraining the impulse to scream, Harriet yanked open the door and fled up the steps. As she reached the top, a shadowy figure appeared in the doorway ahead of her. Moving too fast to stop, Harriet ran straight into the figure, which let out an angry grunt and stumbled backwards.

'Have you gone quite mad?'

The voice was furious. But Harriet recognised it. 'John?' She almost burst into tears with relief. 'Oh, thank God it's you!' In the half light she could see John holding his chest where she had collided with him. She quickly composed herself. 'What are you doing here?'

'What am *I* doing here?' John said incredulously. 'I might ask you the same thing. What the bloody hell are you doing creeping around in here? You can't honestly be that ingenuous. If the owner catches you, you do realise that you could face prosecution for trespass, don't you?'

Harriet wasn't paying any attention. Instead she was tugging at his sleeve. 'John, listen to me, I've seen them down there,' she said breathlessly, waving a hand in the direction of the door at the foot of the steps. 'They spend their days asleep in the cellar.'

'What do you mean by 'they'?' He already knew the answer to that one.

'Those two girls.'

John was having none of it. He grabbed Harriet's arm and pulled her roughly out into the hallway. 'For fuck's sake, woman, let it drop. Now, come on, let's get out of here.'

'It's the truth, I tell you,' Harriet protested. 'Those two

women are down there like the living dead.'

John stopped and turned to face her. 'Oh, so they're the living dead now, are they?' he said sourly.

Suddenly Harriet realised how crazy she must sound. 'Well,' she stuttered, 'one of them at least. I don't know about the other one, but she has to be somewhere close by, from what I've seen they appear to go everywhere together.'

John laughed out loud. 'Just what the hell is this? Sherlock Bailey investigating despicable goings-on in the creepy old manor house? Have you any idea what you sound like? I tell you, my darling, your imagination will be the death of you. Don't forget what happened to the moggy with the inquisitive nature. Come on, let's just go, shall we?'

By the time they got outside, John's anger had almost completely subsided. 'A person's home is sacrosanct, you know,' he said. 'You just can't go wondering around on private property.'

Harriet scoffed, 'There's *nothing* sacrosanct about this place, John, I can assure you. Anyway, how did you find me?'

'Well, there I was preparing you a delicious breakfast, but you didn't return. As the time got on I imagined you'd be sticking your nose in somewhere or other that you shouldn't be. I think we can chalk one up for good old John's intuition there, don't you?'

Harriet linked her arm through his and gave him a squeeze. She decided that further remonstration would probably be futile. And besides, out here in the daylight she had to admit it all seemed rather ridiculous. Just the same, that didn't alter what she had seen. 'You're impossible,' she said, 'but I love you anyway.'

John stopped and took her in his arms. 'And I love you. But this insanity has got to stop, darling.' They kissed. 'Hey, listen, what would you say to shutting up shop and moving on tomorrow morning?'

Harriet's eyes lit up. 'You mean it?'

'Sure.'

'Then I suppose I'd have to say that today would be much better.'

John grinned. 'Yeah, well you would say that, wouldn't you? But seriously, if it will keep you out of court on a charge of breaking and entering then we'll leave. But it's a beautiful morning and I'd like to squeeze in one last day by the lake. Fair enough?'

They kissed again. Harriet smiled. 'Fair enough,' she said, though she wasn't sure that her eyes weren't betraying the fear she still felt over what she had seen in the house.

As they set off arm in arm across the lawn to the caravan, neither one of them was aware that they were being watched from one of the upstairs windows. Someone was banging on the glass trying to attract their attention.

Ted had woken to the sound of voices arguing somewhere off downstairs. Once again Fran had left him alone - no great surprise there - and at first he had thought the voices were in his mind. When they continued, however, one of them getting louder and angrier, he had tried to get off the bed to investigate. Weak and consumed by nausea, he had nonetheless managed to get to his feet. For a minute or two the voices had gone quiet, but now they had resumed and seemed to be coming from outside. He managed to wobble his way over to the window, from where he could see the young couple from the caravan walking across the lawn.

More than ever before Ted had started to realise that his life could be in serious danger. Although it had occurred to him at least twice in the past couple of days, for no other reason than raw lust he had foolishly banished it from his mind. Now he struck the glass with his fist and tried to call out, but all he managed was a strangled moan. There was no chance they would hear him if he didn't apply a little more force, but he simply couldn't find it in himself to do it. He leant back against the wall and sagged to his knees, whereupon he was violently ill.

✲

As dusk once again cast fingers of gloom out across the grounds of Farnsworth Hall, the depressing declaration of an approaching storm rumbled through the thickening clouds.

A short distance away at the roadside a familiar scene was being acted out. Elliot Hatch, the driver of the bright yellow Porsche, could hardly have ignored the two attractive women who flagged him down, could he? He was, after all, a *bon vivant*, a connoisseur of life's luxuries, and a gentleman to the bitter end. At least on face value. And he would certainly never pass up the opportunity to ride gallantly to the aid of a member of the opposite sex in distress. Or, for that matter, to less than gallantly proceed to extract her from her underwear should the chance present itself. Tonight, it seemed, his luck had doubled. The dark-haired woman and her blonde companion climbed into the Porsche and the three of them sped off towards the turning that would lead to Farnsworth Hall and, unbeknownst to Elliot Hatch, the site of his impending execution.

XII

RAVENOUS

Ted's eyes snapped open. He was laid face down on the floor in a puddle of his own stinking vomit. His whole body was white and rancid with sweat, he had a bitch of a headache and a singularly unattractive trail of bile hung from the corner of his mouth. He tried to sit up but his limbs felt leaden and the effort required to do so was too great. 'FRAAAAANN!' he screamed with all the gusto he could muster, but the results were nothing short of feeble. His mind was addled and burgeoning delirium was staving off rational thought. His voice dropped to a whisper. 'Who's there? Outside! I hear voices. Met him. Picked him up. On the roadside no doubt. Just like Rupert... just like *me*!' The panic was building, the true realisation of his situation crunching down on his brain. 'Who are you? Where the hell do you come from?' Ted's haggard features twisted into an ugly grimace. 'Oh, Christ, I must get away from here, I *must* get away before I wind up in the hospital... or the morgue!'

From his position splayed out on the floor, Ted couldn't see Fran. She was standing in the open doorway watching him, listening to his deranged ramblings, a thin smile on her lips. Miriam had been right. It was dangerous to keep this man around any longer. She would make love to him that night for the last time, and then she and her darling Miriam would tear the fucker apart. It would be the best feast ever.

But first there was this other arrogant bastard to attend to.

The bastard in question was, at that very moment, squatted in front of the fireplace, rubbing his hands together in glee, still not quite believing his good fortune. Not only was the scent of sexual intrigue hanging at his nostrils, the beauty of the situation in which he now found himself was that he hadn't even had to exert himself to get here. These two delightful creatures had actually made a play for *him*. But then again, why not? Elliot Hatch was a very attractive man and a fine catch in anyone's book. He chuckled to himself.

They simply couldn't resist you, could they? You old devil, Hatch.

Miriam was attending to some music. The gentle sound of guitar strings drifted from the speaker.

'Ah-ha!' Elliott exclaimed. 'Old world Spain! "Adagio" from the 'The Orange Juice Concerto.' He laughed, delighted at his wit. Miriam stared at him blankly. He coughed to mask the humiliation of the moment. '"Concierto De Aranjuez",' Elliott said. 'Aranjuez... Orange Juice... It's a pun on words, you see.' Miriam evidently didn't see, or if she did then her expression conveyed no amusement.

Okay, it may not be hilarious, but a courtesy smile wouldn't have gone amiss...

Elliott took a stab at retrieving face. 'Actually, Aranjuez refers to an ancient palace outside of Madrid. It was the abode of Spanish kings many years ago. It is a place of immense beauty, much as Rodrigo's composition is one of the most beautiful pieces of music that has ever been written. I commend your excellent taste, my dear.'

'Thank you.' Miriam walked to the table and picked up a bottle of wine. 'Would you like a drink?' she purred.

'Oh, yes, very much indeed,' Elliot said. This was going to be utterly hideous, of that he was convinced. He had yet to find anyone in this Godforsaken country of heathens - the regulars at the Queen's Club graciously excepted, naturally - who could tell a decent Chianti from a vat of vinegar.

Miriam was pouring. 'Say when.'

'Oh, that's plenty, thank you.' Elliot forced a smile of gratitude.

Play it cool, Elliot, old bean, play it cool. A couple of glasses of this cheap plonk and you'll have Barbie-doll here out of her panties.

'FRAAAAANN!'

The scream was so loud that Elliot nearly dropped his glass. He looked around, startled. 'What on earth...?'

Miriam smiled at him sweetly. 'I'm so sorry about that,' she said. 'It's Fran's boyfriend. This always happens when he drinks too much.'

'Oh, really?' Elliot frowned. 'Poor chap. Better luck next time. And, er... speaking of Fran, will the lovely lady not be joining us?'

'Yes, of course. She's just gone to change. If her boyfriend is as drunk as he sounds, she'll be looking for some intelligent company this evening.' Miriam raised her glass. 'Cheers.'

'Yes, cheers.' Steeling himself, Elliot took a sip of the crimson liquid. His eyes widened with astonishment. He had fallaciously expected the worst, but the wine was actually very good. 'This is quite excellent,' he said, unable to disguise his surprise. He took a large mouthful, swilled it around his mouth and allowed it to trickle down his throat. 'It's one of the best wines I've ever tasted,' he added, and meant it.

Affording him a knowing smile that said *I can tell you were expecting something awful, I could see it in your face, but you shouldn't be so quick to pre-judge*, Miriam offered him the bottle. 'Have some more.' Elliot eagerly held out his glass and Miriam refilled it to the brim. 'It's a vintage of our own,' she said. 'My friend and I are rather proud of it.'

Elliot grinned broadly. 'And yet I could tell you everything you could possibly want to know about this wine.'

Miriam feigned awe. 'Oh, really? I don't believe you,' she said.

Elliot was well aware she was patronising him, but that merely added to the fun. With undisguised conceit, he sat upright and said, 'My dear young lady, you are sitting in the presence of a true connoisseur. If you give me a moment I shall begin by identifying the country of origin for you. It shouldn't be too difficult to judge.'

'You'll never guess,' Fran said. Elliot jumped. He hadn't heard her come in. For all his bravura and self-assurance, he was actually a rather timid man who had gone to great lengths to become so well-practiced in the art of exuding

102

confidence and calm.

Fran was standing behind him. 'Golly, I didn't hear you come back,' he laughed nervously.

'Like I say, you'll never guess,' Fran repeated. 'I'll bet you anything you like.'

Elliot quickly regained his equanimity. 'I wouldn't be so sure if I were you,' he chuckled. 'I'm an expert and I've recognised some very obscure wines in my time.'

'Very well,' Fran said, 'let's see how you manage this time.'

Elliot sniffed at his glass. 'Let's see now,' he said. 'We're talking France here, aren't we?'

Fran raised an eyebrow in a non-committal manner. Elliot took a small sip from the glass and sucked it back across his palate. 'Hmmmm, yes, it's a claret.'

Fran scoffed. 'Well, obviously, but...'

'Wait!' Elliot reprimanded her with a wagging finger. If nothing else he could put on a damned impressive show. 'Wait, wait, wait. It comes from a small vineyard. Hmmmm. Well matured. Very well matured in fact.'

Miriam said nothing but continued to sip at her own wine. Fran was enjoying Elliot's performance: 'Go on,' she encouraged him, with a smile that said *You're never going to get this.*

That only served to strengthen Elliot's resolve. He was really into the swing of it now. 'Positive and yet... No, no, no, it's too light. It's definitely not a St. Emilion or a Grave.' He smacked his tongue impatiently against the roof of his mouth. Rodrigo was building to a crescendo, the evocatively delicate sound of guitar melding masterfully with rich, stirring orchestral timbres.

'It's... it's a Médoc. And therefore,' Elliott announced proudly, 'it must be a Margaux.'

He looked hopefully to his hosts for confirmation of his Epicurean aptitude. Both women burst out laughing. Elliot's face fell. 'No? Oh well, er... Pauillac? No, no, no, it's too highly scented, too feminine to be a Pauillac. It's... it's...' He nervously ran his fingers through the forest of tight blonde curls covering his scalp. The pressure was on to nail this little perisher. As excellent as it was, it definitely didn't have the bouquet of a Château Lafite or even a Latour for that matter, though it was unquestionably in the same league as those two princes among wines. 'I've tasted this before,' he continued. 'In the St. Julien region. Yes,' he concluded proudly, 'It's a St. Julien.'

Fran decided that it was time to put him out of his misery. 'Sorry to disappoint you, but you're wrong. This wine comes from a remote part of the Carpathian mountains. She looked at him mockingly as if to say *Call yourself an expert?*

Elliot blinked and stuttered: 'Carpathians?' He cursed himself.

'Yes, that's right,' Fran said. 'It's lucky you didn't have a bet on it, isn't it?'

Elliot tried to conceal his slight embarrassment.

Oh, well done, Hatch. Hardly your most auspicious demonstration to date. They must think you're a proper bloody charlatan now.

'Yes, I suppose it is really,' he said sheepishly. He took another large mouthful and swallowed. 'In any event, it's excellent wherever it's from. What a pity your friend isn't here to appreciate it.' He raised his glass as Fran filled one for herself. 'Cheers,' he grinned.

✳

Outside the rainfall was getting progressively heavier and the skies were hosting an impressive display of light and sound. The wind whipped through the trees and gusted against the side of the little caravan, rocking it on its wheels. Not that Harriet and John were giving it much attention.

Their day had passed quickly. Harriet had finished her excellent painting of Farnsworth Hall and John had spent most of the afternoon dozing beside the lake, returning as dusk fell without so much as a minnow to brandish as a trophy. She had prepared a special dinner - his favourite chicken curry, comprised of the last of the meat she had been able to pack into their small freezer, a tin of Homepride cooking sauce and a packet of inferior but economical Uncle Ben's rice. If her man was going to escort her out of this hellhole tomorrow morning then this evening he was going to be treated like a king.

Harriet was feeling light of heart for the first time in days and didn't even allow the sound of a car passing nearby to distract her too greatly. Just the same, acknowledging to herself the need to sate her innate curiosity, she did take a quick look out of the window. She had seen the two women, accompanied by a dapper looking man in a rather ostentatious check sports coat, going into the house. However, refusing to dwell on the matter, she had immediately returned to preparing the meal. Tomorrow they would be away from here and none of this weirdness would matter any more.

When John had returned they had eaten well and polished off a bottle of Chardonnay between them. Now, with the storm raging outside, John was laid back in bed and Harriet was getting undressed. She was a fine looking woman and watching her disrobe was something John never tired of. She dropped her skirt and then removed her blouse, unclipping her brassiere to reveal the generous breasts that, even after some seven years of familiarity, still held a genuine attraction for him. Stepping out of her panties and kicking them across the floor, Harriet tossed aside the sheets, climbed astride him and gently lowered herself onto his hardness. He reached up and fondled her breasts, finding pleasure in their divine weight. He took each large, dark nipple between a thumb and forefinger and pinched hard. Harriet threw back her head and moaned. She loved it when he did that. John could still recall his surprise upon the initial discovery that his prim and proper young bride - who had unrelentingly refused him full intercourse until after they were married - got her rocks off on mild sadomasochism. It wasn't exactly his bag, but sometimes he could get into it and then sometimes he couldn't.

As Harriet began to grind her damp crotch against him,

so the urgency of his thrusts increased. She rested her hands on his shoulders, pinning him to the bed, and began to raise and lower her hips with heightening speed. John groaned as he felt his glans rubbing up against the soft, burning tissue deep inside her abdomen. 'I love you,' he said.

Harriet bent her head and kissed him. 'Pin me down and fuck me from behind,' she said. 'Now!' She stretched across the bed on all fours and John got to his knees and stroked a finger through the gully that separated the firm, pink buttocks now being offered to him. Then he reached out and, opening a drawer in the bedside cabinet, pulled out two white silk scarves that Harriet had purchased two Christmases ago for this sole purpose. He stretched forward and dangled them in front of her face. Harriet bit her bottom lip and nodded her consent.

Pushing her face down into the pillow, John climbed off the bed and deftly bound each of her arms to the headboard, making sure that there was sufficient room for manoeuvre on her part and that the scarves weren't biting into her wrists. 'Lucky we brought these along,' he grinned.

Climbing back onto the bed behind Harriet's raised posterior, John bent forward and kissed between her legs, tasting the sweet wetness with the tip of his tongue. 'You knows what ya got a-comin' to ya now young miss, don'tcha?' John said in a mock yokel voice.

Harriet giggled, playing along. 'Oh, sir,' she said coyly, 'I'm only an innocent young thing. What are you going to do with that great big pitchfork?'

John brought the flat of his hand down hard on the fleshy curve of her left buttock. Harriet squirmed and squealed with delight. 'A-ha!' he laughed. 'If ya holds still a moment, me young filly, I'll be a-showin' ya!' Again he spanked her, even harder this time, leaving pink finger-marks across his wife's tender rump. Then he positioned the tip of his penis at the wet, fiery entrance to her vagina and thrust his entire length up inside her.

For the next hour their bodies merged, the play-acting dissolving away into a sensitive and tender expression of the love and devotion they held for one another. Later, bathed in the afterglow of their intimacy and heedless of the storm raging outside, they drifted to sleep beneath the warm blankets.

☼

During the hour that John and Harriet were absorbed in giving each other pleasure, Elliot Hatch had found pleasure of his own in the consumption of two bottles of Carpathian wine, and was now feeling a tad light-headed. He hadn't honestly believed Miriam when she had mentioned that there were upwards of a thousand bottles housed in the cellar beneath the house. Regardless, he had followed his hostesses through the maze of corridors, each woman holding a candle to light the way for him. Now, standing beneath the brick arch and surveying the multitude of racks, Elliot was seeing the proof in Miriam's claim. He chuckled in disbelief.

'Well, you certainly *have* got a good stock,' he said. 'You know, I could happily lose myself in here for days.' He walked over to the nearest rack and ran a finger down the row of bottles. He pulled out a 1969 Domaine Courteillac. 'Now that's a beautiful wine,' he muttered approvingly. He sniffed the cork. How he adored that smell, moreover the enticing promise of the potential treat in store that all bottle corks harbour.

Miriam gave a small shrug as if the variety, source and age of a wine didn't interest her one way or the other, just so long as it tasted good. 'I have much better one than that if you'd like to see.'

Elliot nodded. 'Yes, indeed. But better than *this*?' He tapped the Courteillac admiringly and slipped it carefully back into its niche.

'Oh, yes, *much* better.' Miriam smiled. While they had been perusing the racks, Fran had settled herself at the table. She lit a cigarette and sat back smoking it, watchful and silent as Miriam led Elliot through the cluster of racks, pausing every so often as the self-professed connoisseur stooped randomly to pull out a bottle. Blowing away the dust, he inspected each label before sliding the bottle back into place and moving on.

They reached the end of an aisle and Miriam extracted a bottle herself, seductively pursed her lips and blew away the dust. She handed the bottle to Elliot. 'Here.'

He accepted it from her and saw that it was a 1955 Mouton Rothschild. Elliot was astounded. 'That's *fantastic*!' he exclaimed. He simply had to taste it. So much so that, were it to come down to a choice between sampling the Mouton or getting intimate with his hostesses, it would definitely be a case of 'Goodnight ladies'. Of course, he was hoping that both options were on the menu. And the way things were shaping up he could see no reason why he wouldn't be partaking of more wine and the pleasures of the flesh too before the night was through. 'You know,' he hinted broadly, 'this really is the sort of wine I appreciate.'

'We tend to save it for our most special guests,' Miriam teased.

'My dear girl,' Elliot retorted, 'I'll have you know that guests don't come any more special than Mr. Elliot Hatch.'

Another hour passed, at the end of which the special Mr. Elliot Hatch was well and truly inebriated. He was sitting between the two women at the table which was now cluttered with empty bottles. 'You know,' he giggled, 'we really should have allowed this splendid elixir to breathe for a few minutes before we imbibed. And as for correct room temperature, well... it's bloody freezing down here.'

Both Fran and Miriam had been drinking in moderation, quite content to permit their guest to ingest from their stock in liberal quantities. Chuckling for no particular reason, Elliot refilled the goblets on the table and swallowed another large draught. 'When I tell the chaps about this, they just won't believe it,' he slurred. 'An isolated house in the woods at the witching hour of -' he hiccuped, apparently having some difficulty in getting the words out '- of midnight, in a shellar... a cellar full of marvellous wine, and... and above all else, in the company of two very charming young ladies.' He shook his head. 'It's almost too good to be true.'

Miriam set down her goblet. 'Nothing's too good to be true,' she said. 'The only trouble is life's too short. Each of us owes a death, you know. It's just that for some pay day comes a lot sooner than for others.'

In a sober state Elliot might have found her comment odd, but right now he wasn't even really listening. He was too wrapped up in his own little world, wrestling with the problem of how best to separate these two tasty little trollops from their underwear. He glanced bleary-eyed at his watch. 'That's damned strange,' he mumbled. 'My watch has stopped.' He held out his wrist as if it were necessary to prove it. 'Look. That's never happened before.' He shook it, failing to notice the look that passed between Fran and Miriam.

Fran stood up and walked around the table. She stood between Elliot and Miriam, delivering to each of them in turn a long, sensual kiss. Elliot was delighted. He had read about situations such as this in the letters pages of "Mayfair" magazine, but had always taken them with a pinch of salt. But God be damned if he wasn't actually living out one of those divine sounding little fantasies right now. He found the prospect of a threesome deliciously arousing.

Fran took a sip of wine and, kissing Elliot again, passed it from her mouth into his. He hadn't expected that. Coughing and laughing at the same time he sprayed dark liquid across the front of Fran's gown. 'Ooops... sorry.' He clumsily tried to wipe it off but when he attempted to stand he discovered that his legs had deserted him. He dropped heavily back into the chair and satisfied himself with watching Miriam and Fran embrace. Scrabbling at the straps on Fran's gown, all he managed to do was tear it. The material ripped aside and one of her lusciously plump bosoms tumbled free. Miriam sat back and watched as Fran allowed the vile little man to unceremoniously paw at her breasts. But when Elliot began to chew on one of Fran's nipples Miriam decided enough was enough. She looked at Fran and nodded. It was time.

Twisting Elliot's tie around her fist, Fran yanked him to

his feet and kissed him again. Startled at first by her ferocity, he returned the kiss and then pushed her aside, greedily lurching towards Miriam. 'Your turn, sweet cheeks,' he slurred. That was the moment Miriam struck. Ducking to avoid his slobbering mouth, she jabbed her head forward like a coiled viper and bit deeply into the bristled flesh of his throat. Elliot let out a high-pitched squeal and tottered backwards against the wall, eyes wide with terror and clutching at his injured neck. He looked down in disbelief at his hand. It was wet and red. 'What...? Why....? I don't understand...'

Miriam was grinning, showing blood - *his* blood - smeared across her perfect white teeth. Fran was standing beside her, staring at him, the tip of her tongue flicking across her lips. 'Oh, Christ,' he snivelled. 'No...'

Suddenly, from out of nowhere, Fran had a knife in her hand and was rushing at him. Elliot tried hopelessly to dodge the first strike, but the blade sank deep into his shoulder and passed out through the other side. He screamed again as Fran twisted the long, curved edge, ripping through the deltoid muscle as she worked it free. Elliot crumpled to the floor, blood pouring from his shoulder. Like a wounded animal he scuttled on all fours across the flagstones, crashing headlong into a rack of wine. There was a dull crack as his skull encountered the solid wood and several bottles tumbled down around him and smashed on the floor. One struck him on the temple and his vision blacked for a few seconds. Head swimming, he reached out blindly and managed to grasp hold of the rack. With an almighty effort he hoisted himself to his feet and, as his vision came back, he turned to meet his fate.

'Right, just back off!' he screamed, adopting a pitifully inept kung fu stance he'd once seen in a Bruce Lee movie. Panting and drooling like ravenous, rabid dogs, his attackers didn't falter for an instant. Instead Miriam lashed out a hand and her sharp nails gouged out a clump of meat from the back of Elliot's fingers. Whimpering and clutching at it with his other hand to try and staunch the flow of blood, he dropped to his knees amidst the broken glass, feeling several pieces of the debris embed themselves in his legs. Sobbing with pain, he held out his arms in a plea for mercy. The knife in Fran's hand flashed out twice more, expertly debilitating the biceps in both arms and rendering him practically helpless. His lifeblood was spurting out from the deep lacerations and there was nothing Elliot could do to stop it. In that moment he felt the icy breath of the harbinger of death on his neck. Folding his invalid arms across his chest, his once crisp white shirt now stained dark, he toppled sideways onto the floor and curled himself into the foetal position. In an instant both women were upon him, finger-nails tearing, teeth snapping, tongues lapping, like feral beasts that hadn't seen food in days. They tore off strips of flesh and gristle, sucking out the red nourishment and then spitting the chewed-up remnants on the floor.

Had he been asked ten minutes earlier what his preferred mode of passing into the next world might be, Elliot would undoubtedly have replied that there could be no better way than to greet death brimming with the finest vino and in the arms of a beautiful woman. Two even. He could not, however, have had the slightest inclination of just how hideous a way to die that might actually be. Now he was finding out. He had always been a firm believer in the adage that, at the moment of death, your life passes before you. Yet as he lay there on the floor of the cellar awaiting the picture-book cascade of images of his childhood to begin, bizarrely the only thing he saw was the appallingly sentimental lyric to the Terry Jacks song "Seasons in the Sun".

'Goodbye my friend, it's hard to die'...

Moments later those too were gone, lost in blinding whiteness as he surrendered himself to the inevitable. An instant before his throat was completely torn out, he said - or at least thought he did - 'How *bloody* banal.'

And then Elliot Hatch, owner of a successful accountancy firm in Marylebone, a not insubstantial bank balance and a brand new shiny Porsche, was dead.

FINAL DESTINATION

How Ted Gorman managed to get himself into a pair of trousers and a shirt, then negotiate his way down the corridors and stairwells to get from the bedroom to the downstairs hall - let alone stagger blindly across the grounds of Farnsworth to the sanctuary of Harriet and John's caravan - was beyond explanation. In a state of mind that verged on insanity, coupled with the agonising cramps that raged in his bones, it was surprising that he'd even harnessed the will-power to get up off the floor. And yet, tapping into that hidden reserve that has been known to surface from deep within man in life threatening circumstances, Ted *had* managed it.

It was John who opened the door to investigate the faint knocking sound, though he wouldn't have even been aware of it if not for Harriet shaking him out of a rather unpleasant dream. He had been standing on a sun terrace beside a hotel swimming pool filled with vivid blue water. It looked cool and inviting and he could feel the sweat trickling down the back of his neck. As he started to walk around the perimeter of the pool, the terrace grew narrower until it was no more than eight inches wide. Rather than go back, he pressed himself back against the wall of the hotel trying to retain his balance. When he looked down he saw that the water had become discoloured; the vivid blue was gone, in its place a murky red that reminded him of a jar of pickled beets, except that instead of the vegetable he loathed he could see gnarled roots and prickly branches lurking just below the surface. As he tried to edge along the wall he lost his footing and pitched forward into the frightening morass. He tried to swim back to the side but the branches conspired to prevent him from doing so, latching on to his legs as if they were alive, and dragging him under. It was as the putrid water started to fill his lungs that Harriet had come to his rescue.

'John, there's someone outside the door. I can hear banging.'

Grateful to have been plucked from his nightmare and deposited back into reality, John got out of bed. Wiping the sweat from his forehead with the back of his hand, he reasoned that the dream had most likely been the product of the curry and Chardonnay coupled with the strenuous *aprés dejeuner* activity. 'I didn't hear anything,' he said. Pulling on his trousers, he padded to the door. 'However, just for you, I'll have a quick...' The sentence was left unfinished as a faint banging sound reached his ears. He looked back at Harriet, who was sitting up in bed with the covers pulled up around her. 'Hang on, I heard *that*,' he said. Sliding back the latch, John opened the door a couple of inches and peered out through the gap. 'My God!' he exclaimed, yanking it wide open.

Someone was laying face down in the mud directly in front of the door. One of the arms was stretched up, resting limply across the step. What appeared to be dirty hand marks at the base of the door explained the banging sound. John wondered how long the poor devil had been trying to get their attention.

He jumped down and knelt beside the body. Rolling it over, in spite of the grime, he immediately recognised the visage of the man who had come seeking assistance a few days beforehand. 'Quick, darling,' he called to Harriet, 'get some clothes on. It's that Ted chap from the other day and he looks in pretty bad shape.'

Ted's eyelids fluttered open and he tried to mouth 'Help me', but no sound came out. It was a bit of a struggle, but John managed to haul him up onto his feet, by which time Harriet had appeared in the doorway behind him. She was wearing a diaphanous nightgown that left nothing to the imagination and which, at any other time, John would have taken immense pleasure in extricating her from. Between the pair of them they managed to get Ted - who had now

113

completely lost consciousness - up through the door and over to the bed.

While John gathered some blankets from the closet and laid them over the prone body, Harriet quickly filled a bowl with some hot water and began sponging the mud off the injured man's face. She was startled by the pasty whiteness lurking beneath. 'He looks in pretty poor shape, John,' she said with a discernible tremor in her voice. 'He's so white. It's almost as if he's been drained of blood. What should we do?'

John was pouring a glass of whisky. 'Here, give him this.'

Harriet took the glass and pushed it to Ted's lips, trying to get some of the amber fluid into his mouth. But it dribbled down his chin and splashed onto the bedclothes. 'This is no good,' she said. 'I think we ought to get him to a hospital.'

John didn't at all relish the idea of trying to get the car down the mud track in the dark, let alone driving around trying to locate a hospital in this neck of the woods in the middle of the night. But one look at Ted's ashen face and he had to agree; without medical aid this man was on his way to the pearly gates. 'Yeah, you're right,' he said, pulling on his socks. 'I'll unhitch the car and get her started. You stop here and look after him. And for God's sake keep the door shut. I shan't be long, then you'll have to help me get him into the car.'

It took John less than three minutes to unchain and separate the ball and socket nexus and disconnect the lighting cable to the caravan. He glanced up at the night sky which was now clear and filled with a fantastic vista of twinkling stars. 'At least it's stopped raining for five minutes,' he muttered to himself. Opening the car door, he climbed in and slotted the key into the ignition.

An angry hissing sound to his left made him turn his head and he physically jumped at the sudden appearance of Miriam outside the passenger window. Her eyes were wild, her blonde locks tousled, her pretty face speckled with what John didn't hesitate to recognise as blood. Harriet's voice echoed in his mind: '...almost as if he's been drained of blood.' Before John could react, there was a snarl from the back seat behind him and a strong arm slithered around his neck and held him in a headlock. Miriam already had the passenger door open and as John struggled to free himself from Fran's grip, her other arm came into view in front of his face. For a fleeting moment his brain registered that the hand was holding a knife. And then, with a single swift downward motion, the blade sheared off the end of John's nose. He opened his mouth to scream and threw up his left hand over the oozing remains of his ravaged proboscis. The knife swooped in on its second assault, this time taking off his index finger and a part of his thumb. Eyes wide and head lolling as a wave of nausea overcame him, John shakily held up his injured hand in front of his face, watching with curious fascination as the blood departed his veins in uneven pulsing squirts like water from a garden hose with a kink in it.

Miriam pounced and seized his wrist with a strength that her slender frame belied. She pulled his hand to her mouth and closed her lips over the pumping stumps, sucking and swallowing with unrestrained relish. Grabbing a clump of John's hair in her hand, Fran began to shake his head back and forth and from side to side, much as a lioness will worry into submission the dying gazelle she's about to devour. Then she violently yanked his head hard back against the headrest. John's feet were kicking aimlessly against the brake and accelerator pedals as very slowly, with consummate precision, Fran drew the razor-sharp blade horizontally across his throat. A fine red line beaded up in its wake, widening as she pulled back his head further still and applied her mouth to the flowing haemoglobin.

Strength dissipating rapidly, John vainly attempted to pull his left hand away from Miriam's mouth whilst desperately trying to claw away Fran's head from his throat with his right. He jerked around helplessly in the seat, but the increasing blood loss was beginning to make him dizzy. With little resistance Miriam was able to pull him sideways so that his head dropped into her lap. Fran, licking her stained lips, handed her lover the knife. She accepted it and, as if there was all the time in the world, used the flat of the blade to pop the buttons from John's shirt. Now he was gurgling, starting to choke on his own blood. One flailing arm caught the indicator switch and, as the light on the dashboard blinked into life, the bleeding stumps of his thumb and index finger painted the interior of the windscreen with a red wash.

Running the tip of the blade through the dark, matted hairs on John's chest, Miriam allowed it to come to rest at his navel. John looked up into the blue eyes which were coruscating with hatred and the thrill of the kill, and then he felt the pressure, followed by a stinging pain, as the blade slid home. With a powerful wrench upwards, Miriam slit him open from the belly to the bottom of his ribcage. Involuntarily he began to thrash from side to side, for now he had little in the way of self-control; the automatic pilot that is the instinct of self-preservation had taken firm hold of the reins. But Fran was already climbing over from the back seat. She sat down astride him and, with her full weight pressed down upon him and blackness enveloping his vision, he had no option but to submit. Gradually the thrashing subsided and he lay still.

Taking hold of either side of the grotesque slit Miriam had opened in John's torso, Fran peeled him open, exposing the lower ribs and many of his vital organs. Then she dipped her hands into the gaping cavity, ecstatically feeling her way through the soft, warm entrails. After probing around for a few moments, she withdrew and, putting one hand to her own mouth, she held out the other to her lover. Miriam leant forward and fastidiously licked and sucked away the blood and winkled out the tiny fragments of flesh from under the fingernails. Together they fed until Fran's hands were as good as clean.

Then they got out of the car, linked arms, and casually walked away towards the edge of the trees. John's murder had taken them no more than two minutes. And, although it had been customarily messy, the women had executed it

116

with such stealth and skill that Harriet, back inside the caravan, had heard nothing.

Whilst awaiting for John's return she had sat herself on the edge of the bed beside Ted and applied a cool compress to his brow. Although she wouldn't swear to it, already it looked to her as if a little colour had returned to the anaemic features. Ted had even regained partial consciousness and was mumbling to himself. Much of what he said was incoherent, but what little Harriet was able to decipher chilled her to the bone. 'Blood. No accident. Murder. MURDER! Got to get away. I'm next.' The more she listened the more frightened she became, as the shadowy fears that had haunted her since their arrival at this spot gelled into something terrifyingly real. Unable to sit still any longer, she got up and went to the window.

What the hell is the man doing? How long does it take to start a bloody car?

Unable to see anything, she draped an overcoat across her shoulders, opened the door and cautiously looked out. There was no sign of her husband, but the right-hand indicator on the Wolseley was flashing. Harriet took a hesitant step down into the mud. 'John?' Nothing. She called again, more frantic now.

Her eyes darting nervously back and forth, she scurried over to the car and pulled open the door, promptly reeling away at the sight of her eviscerated husband stretched out across the seats. 'Oh, God, John! Noooooo!' The coat dropped from her shoulders and she stumbled backwards against the side of the caravan, lost her balance and crashed down into the mud, sobbing uncontrollably.

From out of the darkness Fran and Miriam came rushing towards her, talons extended, teeth bared, hot breath steaming from their nostrils, snarling like rabid dogs. Before Harriet could even comprehend what was happening, the women had effortlessly pulled her up on her feet and were dragging her kicking and screaming across the grass towards the house. The harder she struggled the more iron the grip on her arms became until the realisation finally

117

registered that escape wasn't going to be that easy. It would have to be timed just right. She let herself go limp, but the two women comfortably handled the change in body weight and between them they carried Harriet into the house and down to the cellar. There they cast her roughly onto the floor.

When she felt the unpleasant sensation of wetness seeping through her flimsy gown, Harriet's first thought was that it must be the mud from where she had fallen outside the caravan. But as she rolled over onto her side, to her horror she saw that the floor was awash with blood and intestines. A few feet away against the wall lay the crumpled remains of a body. Harriet began to scream but Miriam bent forward and slapped her hard across the side of the face. 'Shut the fuck up you little bitch!' Then, in the blink of an eye, she had manoeuvred round behind Harriet and grabbed her by the wrists. Forcing her up onto her knees, she pinned her arms firmly behind her.

'Shush, shush, darling,' Fran was saying, stepping up in front of Harriet. 'Please don't cry.' The tone was so comforting that Harriet's sobs abruptly receded to a snivel and she looked up into the jubilant face. 'My friend Miriam tells me that you were looking at my body while I was asleep, is that right?' The voice was hypnotic and, as had happened upon her first encounter with Fran, Harriet felt the fear drain from her. She nodded slowly. 'And did you like what you saw, little one?'

As she spoke, Fran was unbuttoning her gown, which Harriet noticed was covered with dark, wet patches of... of blood. John's blood. She began to shake and the intensity of her sobs increased again.

Miriam said angrily, 'Fran, we haven't got time for this now.'

'There's time,' Fran said calmly. She finished disrobing and moved up close to Harriet so that her crotch was only inches away from her face. Harriet caught the warm, tangy scent of Fran's womanhood. The captor gazed down gloatingly at the captive. 'Wouldn't you like to taste?' she said. 'Aren't you just a little curious?' Harriet kept her head bowed. 'Ahh, yes,' Fran continued, 'but we should remember what curiosity did to the cat.'

John's very words.

Oh, God, John. My poor John...

With unexpected suddenness Harriet lunged forward and before Miriam could stop her she had sunk her teeth in the soft flesh of Fran's thigh.

Fran screamed. 'Bitch!' Eyes blazing she looked at Miriam. 'Strip her!'

With a single tug Miriam tore away the flimsy nightgown, leaving Harriet cowering on the floor. Her body was shining with sweat. Cold sweat. The sort of sweat born of stark terror that one only ever reads about in horror stories but that can't possibly be real. Only this was very real.

Miriam produced the knife from the folds of her cape and handed it to Fran. Then she again grabbed hold of Harriet's arms and pinned them back in a vice-like grip. Still naked, Fran squatted down in front of Harriet, who took the opportunity to spit in the woman's face.

Fran was unfazed. 'It could have been something so very special,' she said. She looked past Harriet and raised an eyebrow at Miriam who was glowering with unconcealed jealousy. 'But now...'

Harriet felt the tip of the blade prod against her left breast just above the nipple. 'You killed my husband, you fucking whore,' she managed to blurt out through her sobs.

Fran smiled sadistically and nodded. 'And now I'm going to kill you too.' She leaned so that her full weight was behind the hilt of the dagger and it slid forward, burying itself deep in Harriet's breast.

Harriet let out a terrible scream and Miriam giggled with excitement. 'Again, Fran, again...' Fran withdrew the knife and as it cleared the entry wound blood welled out behind it. Harriet was moaning, her head bowed low as she fought to deal with the searing pain. Through her half-closed eyes she could see the bloody teeth marks in Fran's thigh and that strengthened her resolve.

'You should know that I'm really good at this, darling,'

Fran was saying. 'If you'd played along I could have made it sweet and painless for you. Instead it's going to be drawn out and exquisitely painful. I would say that this is going to hurt me more than it'll hurt you.' She laughed aloud. 'But then that would make me a liar.' A sadistic smile lit up her face and she traced the tip of the dagger around the relief of Harriet's nipple. Suddenly she turned it on its edge and with a vicious downwards slicing motion Harriet's nipple parted company with the bulbous formation of her breast. Harriet threw back her head and screamed as she had never screamed in her life before. She struggled to break free of Miriam's grasp but it was unyielding.

Her head dropped forward again. Now she knew with certainty that there would be no escape for her. No last minute reprieve. She was going to die and that was that. It was just a case of how long it would be until the blessed relief of unconsciousness transported her away from this ghastly nightmare.

Fran set down the blood-spattered knife and with great care took the bleeding mammary between her hands. Then she put her mouth to it and began to drink, like an infant suckling on its mother. Harriet's blood tasted wonderful and Fran swooned as it flowed down her throat in thick crimson gulps.

'Fran!' Miriam said urgently. 'This is taking too long. We have to deal with Ted before he gets away.'

Reluctantly Fran pulled her bloodied mouth away from Harriet's breast. 'There's no rush. He's incapacitated.'

'But for how long? You didn't think he had the strength to get out of the house in the first place.'

There was a moment's silence. Then Fran said, 'You're right.'

She placed a hand under Harriet's chin and raised her head, gently dabbing the tears away with the end of her extended middle finger. She moved in close so that her lips brushed against Harriet's ear. Harriet could feel the heat of the whisper that delivered her epitaph: 'Consider yourself fortunate, you little bitch.' Then she kissed Harriet very softly on the lips and quickly drew the blade across her white throat. It opened up like an over-ripe piece of fruit and the vital juices gushed out. Miriam let go of Harriet's arms and her lifeless body dropped to the floor like a stone.

HAROLD AND MAUDE

Francesca and Miriam ran like the wind. The first light was nosing through the treetops as they rushed back across the grassy stretch towards the caravan. By the time they reached the door the pair of them were out of breath. Fran was the first inside, ready at last to take the life of the man who had taken hers. She looked desperately around the small living quarters.

Where is he? WHERE IS HE?!

She whirled around to face Miriam.

'Look!' Miriam cried, pointing towards the rear window. Fran pressed her hands to the glass in dismay. Several hundred yards away, stumbling across the mossy ground, Ted had almost reached his car. In a matter of moments he would climb inside and drive away and there was nothing that either of them could do to prevent it.

Miriam rested a hand on Fran's shoulder. 'We must go now.'

Fran looked at her fearfully. 'But we can't let him get away alive!' she sobbed. 'He killed me. He killed us. If it weren't for him we wouldn't be cursed with this hellish existence. He has to die!' She stared into Miriam's eyes, her face etched with regret and tacit apology.

I'm so sorry, my darling. You were right and I was wrong. Please tell me how I can make everything right again.

Miriam's voice was steady, controlled. 'It's too late. It's getting light. We must go now.' She took Fran's hand and led her to the door. 'At least we shall spend eternity together.'

In the doorway they paused and embraced. And then they began to run; across the grounds of Farnsworth Hall - now bathed in the red glow of a morning sky that threatened more rain - and through the line of trees that bordered the dense woods. A whorl of leaves flew up behind them like the trail of foam left in the wake of a speeding vessel, and then settled again as if no-one had ever been there to disturb them.

※

'Hey there!'

The plummy voice was jarringly loud and very annoyed.

Ted opened his eyes. He was behind the wheel of his car on the gravel forecourt of Farnsworth Hall. He looked round in the direction of the voice which was saying, irritably, 'Are you listening to me? Farnsworth is private property and you have no right to be parked here. Damn and blast it, it's simply unacceptable. Didn't you read the notice on the road back there? Are you blind?'

Ted was disoriented. The man leaning into the passenger window of the BMW was becoming angrier by the moment. 'Oh, come along, wake up! I'm not renowned for my patience.' Ted looked at him. A checked cloth cap shadowed the face a little, but not so much so that he couldn't make out the small, piggy eyes, the flushed, ruddy cheeks and the whispy white moustache that had been meticulously waxed into an upward curl at either end. 'Be thankful I don't run you in, you blighter. Drinking *and* trespass. You buggers are always the same. Next time go and drink your wine somewhere else.'

Wine?

Ted looked down at the passenger seat, upon which lay two empty bottles. He stammered, 'No, wait a minute, let me explain. I...'

The man cut him dead. 'I'm not the least bit interested in your pathetic explanations. The best thing you can do is move on. I've work to do and your presence here is hardly an asset.'

Ted was suddenly aware of two other people loitering in the background about twenty yards away. An old man and an old woman. Their attire spoke of great wealth and they were both looking impatiently towards the arsehole who was scolding Ted.

123

'Wait. Please wait just a moment,' Ted implored. His mind was reeling. 'What day is it? I have to know. Please. What's the date?'

'The date?' the arsehole spluttered gruffly. He was staring at Ted as if he were wondering whether this drunken lout were daft as well as blind. 'Are you trying to tell me that you've drunk so much that you don't even know what day of the week it is?'

'Please...'

'It's Wednesday of course. Wednesday the 16th of October.' The tone became threatening. 'Now I'm warning you for the last time. Get your sorry backside off this property right now.'

The man turned away and strutted confidently over to the elderly couple. Ted stared after him.

'Is there a problem here Mr. Kenchington-Smythe?' the old man asked. The accent was unmistakably American. Texan in fact.

'No, no, no, Mr. Bick,' the arsehole blustered. 'Just some itinerant sot who strayed past the private property signs. Nothing to worry about. I've given him a piece of my mind, he'll be on his way in a minute.'

Ted looked at his watch. It was working perfectly. 9.18 in the morning on Wednesday the 16th of October. But it couldn't be. The last thing Ted could remember with any clarity was sitting in his room at the Wayfarer Inn. But that had been several days ago... hadn't it? His eyes were brimming with tears. No, it hadn't. Last night. It was last night. But then that would mean...

A dream. A terrible, terrible dream! But no, surely it can't have been...

Everything had seemed so real. The girls. The house. Those Bailey people. Ted looked over towards where the caravan had been. It wasn't there.

All so real...

Fearful of what he might find, Ted rolled up the sleeve of his shirt. Where he expected to see the ugly gash in the crook of his arm there was nothing.

124

All so real...

Given that it had all been a dream - and Ted wasn't sure how it possibly could have been - what in God's name had possessed him to come out here in the first place? *God's* name? God didn't come into it. That he had been so drunk as to have no recollection whatsoever of leaving the hotel, let alone driving out to Farnsworth, was the work of Satan.

Ted could hear Kenchington-Smythe talking. 'The price being asked for the house is cheap if you consider the amount of land it's standing on.'

The elderly man interjected. 'What Maude... er, my wife and I would really like to know is if there is any truth in the legend that they tell about this old house.'

Kenchington-Smythe chuckled. 'Well, it's true that the place has a history of ill fortune. Most recently, just a few years ago in fact, the bodies of two young women were found, the owner of the house and her, er... her, er...' he cleared his throat, embarrassed, 'well, let's say a female companion. It's a sad story that hasn't really helped in selling the house. You know how superstitious people can be. And you know what they say about murderers. How they become haunted by or perhaps even remorseful of their grave misdemeanours and always find themselves compelled to return to the scene of the crime. Utter stuff and nonsense, naturally. As I am sure is the belief in the village that the ghosts of the two poor women haunt the building.'

Trying to rationalise the manner in which the subconscious mind orchestrates the dream state is an impossible task. But it's a hard fact that something as insignificant as a dream can change the manner in which one views the world, casting a whole new perspective upon reality. Three years had passed without so much as a tear shed, not a single pang of guilt over the terrible thing Ted had done. At first there had been fear at the prospect of being caught, for sure. But not guilt, never that.

In a moment of epiphany the remorse washed over him in tumultuous waves. Only now did it occur to him that he hadn't even known the Miriam girl. She had been nothing more to Ted than a name. Perhaps not knowing her had made it easier. After all, he had been so enraged when Fran walked out on him to shack up with another woman - a lesbian lover no less! - that sanity and morality had been buried beneath a burning desire for revenge. And so he'd made them both pay. Until now he'd thought what he'd done had been right - on the rare moments when he even bothered to think about it at all that is. But what on earth had made him believe that he had had the right to mete out such a warped interpretation of justice? Now he thought that it might have been better if everything *had* been real and he had paid the only true penalty for murder: Death. Now that would be fair. *That* would be justice.

Ted began to weep. 'Fran. Oh, God, Fran, I'm *so* sorry.'

He had shut it all out completely. His mind had jumped the rails and he had buried himself in work. That had been wrong. He knew that now, with such clarity in fact that he wondered how he hadn't seen it before. Something he had read as a child popped into his mind. It was a line pertaining to the disappearance of Ichabod Crane in the Washington Irving novella "The Legend of Sleepy Hollow". It went something like: 'As he was a bachelor and in nobody's debt, nobody troubled his head any more about him.' Ted had always thought how awful it must be to die without anyone ever noticing you were gone. He was now all too painfully aware that, much like old Ichabod Crane, if he, Ted Gorman, were to have been snatched by death that day, there was no-one in the world who would have mourned his passing. There were no friends - at least not true friends - no family and no loved ones. The only person he had ever really felt love for he had murdered. Perhaps having to live with that knowledge made for even more fitting a punishment than death itself.

Of course, the all-consuming hurt and confusion he felt right now would fade with the passing of the years. But the memory of Fran and Miriam and the terrible thing he had done would continue to gnaw at his soul for the rest of his days.

Kenchington-Smythe, who it was reasonable to surmise was an estate agent, was still waffling away: 'One can't believe in such things as ghosts nowadays, can one?'

The hard-sell appeared to be working, for the elderly man said, with evident excitement, 'Maude and I would be thrilled at the idea of having a ghost in the place. Just imagine the informal weekends here.'

The old woman pulled up her mink stole around her ears. 'Oh, Harold, darling, isn't this all fascinating? We can't possibly miss this opportunity.'

Kenchington-Smythe clapped his hands together with delight. 'You're making the right decision. You won't regret it.'

Ted pulled out a handkerchief, mopped away his tears and blew his nose. He cast a final look at the quirky trio, who were making their way off around the side of the building, then he turned the key in the ignition and the BMW's engine growled into life.

Neither Ted nor the estate agent - nor, for that matter, the affluent American couple that he was so preoccupied with trying to impress - had noticed the movement in one of the upstairs windows of the house. A woman was standing holding aside the curtain, watching the proceedings in the grounds below. The morning light touched on the highlights in her dark, chestnut-coloured hair. The face was pale, with large doe eyes and a generous mouth that curled into a humourless smile. Then she stepped away into the darkness of the room and the curtain fell back into place.

Pressing down on the accelerator, Ted executed a swift u-turn and set off towards the track that led to the road upon which he would begin the journey towards the rest of his life. He had no idea right now what the future might hold in store for him. But of one thing he had no doubt: Whatever path it may weave, the man walking it would never be quite the same person again.

Tim Greaves first saw 'Vampyres' in the early 1980s. Some years on he interviewed members of the cast and crew for a self-published book devoted to the film's minutiae. With his enthusiasm still burning bright, he has now turned the film into his first novelisation.

Tim is employed full time by an international publishing company and fills his spare time pursuing an affinity for freelance film journalism. He has conducted interviews and written articles for many magazines worldwide, including *Shivers, Femme Fatales* (on which he served a period as British Correspondent), *Little Shoppe of Horrors* and *Uncut,* as well as self-publishing a number of his own genre-related journals. He has also supplied research and written work for several books, among them *Ten Years of Terror: British Horror Films of the 1970s* (FAB Press, 2001) and *Flesh & Blood Book One* (FAB Press, 1998).

Tim lives in the south of England and has been married to Sara since 1984. They have a daughter, Kirsten.